Boys in the Club

Boys in the Club

M.T. Pope

www.urbanbooks.net

Urban Books, LLC
300 Farmingdale Road, NY-Route 109
Farmingdale, NY 11735

ISBN 13: 978-1-64556-645-8

First Mass Market Printing August 2024
First Trade Paperback Printing January 2023
Printed in the United States of America

10 9 8 7 6 5 4 3 2 1

Distributed by Kensington Publishing Corp.
Submit Orders to:
Customer Service
400 Hahn Road
Westminster, MD 21157-4627
Phone: 1-800-733-3000
Fax: 1-800-659-2436

Boys in the Club

by

M.T. Pope

It is said that all work and no play makes life dull. This is exactly the way my four best friends—named Justin, Keith, Marcus, and Evan—think. These young guys are four diligent professionals who have an addiction to club life.

Keith is in the banking field and is trying to rise to the top as easily as possible, but it is not happening as fast as he would like.

Justin is a caregiver with a heart of gold. He loves taking care of the needs of his patients, but he is on a search for someone to take care of his needs.

Marcus is a therapist with great wisdom and impeccable honesty. He owns his own business, and it is doing well. His life seems perfect, but his work life is boring him to tears.

Evan is the handsome hunk of the bunch. He is a personal trainer and will whip you into shape with ease, but his own life is in shambles.

Partying hard gets easier to do with these guys as the pressures of life get the best of them. Drinking, bad decisions, and bad boys are always a recipe for disaster. Club life seems like the perfect escape, but will it ruin their lives?

Books by *M.T. Pope*

Novels

Both Sides of the Fence 1
Both Sides of the Fence 2
Both Sides of the Fence 3
Both Sides of the Fence 4
A Clean Up Man
May the Best Man Win
Hustling on the Down Low
Trouble in Rio w/Carl Weber

Anthologies

Don't Ask Don't Tell
M.T. Pope Presents: Boys Will Be Boys
Anna J Presents: Erotic Snapshots, Volume 1

Novellas

Lost Pages of Both Sides of the Fence, Volume 1
Stick Up Boys

Short Stories

"Don't Drop the Soap"
"Santa's Little Helper"

Acknowledgments

Wow . . . Look at God.

It's been a minute since my last full-length novel. This is my ninth novel and my fifteenth publication. What a miracle it is to finish another book. As usual for me, it was a labor of love. I want to thank God for creativity and endurance. I want to thank Urban Books and Carl Weber for another opportunity. Finally, I want to thank my natural and spiritual family for pushing and prodding me to get this done, along with other things in my life. Until the next one . . .

Peace and Blessings.

Prologue

Death's Door

There was a quiet in the room that matched the urgency of the current circumstances. It was cold and still. There were machines beeping and tubes running in and out of holes in his body. None of us could have imagined this scene before us right now. One of our friends was knocking on death's door.

Fear and pain had taken away our speech, but the tears flowed freely. We looked at each other with the unspoken hope and the blatant fear that were undoubtedly racing in our hearts and minds.

I wondered what we could have done to prevent this.

We all were standing close to the door, threatening to run out of the room. I wanted someone to pinch, punch, or slap me to awaken me from this nightmare. No one moved. I couldn't. I just stared at the sight before me. Selfishly, I was glad that it wasn't me. I was not ready to die. But I knew that my friend in that bed felt the same way. I was praying to God for a miracle. I was not a praying man, but I was hoping that God heard me loud and clear. It was his call, though. I was not naive in that area. I knew who was in charge of it all.

It seemed like an eternity, but we had been there for only a few minutes. My body involuntarily started to tremble. Someone grabbed my hand to calm me down. The warmth of that palm on mine eased my mind.

I was going to be the brave one. I willed myself to move. With one step in front of the other, I walked toward that bed. My heart was thumping, my mind racing, but I did it.

I reached out and placed my hand on his hand as it lay beside his body. It was warm. It gave me hope. I needed it. I felt like God was answering my prayers. Soon the others followed. They did the same thing, reached for his hand. We all held on to him, hoping that this wasn't the last time that we felt his warmth.

Memories of us at the club flooded my mind. The laughs. The cries. The fights. The cursing each other out. The raunchy talks.

I was gripping it all in my mind. And my prayers to God felt akin to the police beating on the door in the middle of the night. Right now I wanted His full attention when it came to my friend. I needed

Him to answer me. I needed my friend to make it. I willed it with all of me. I just needed Him to agree with me.

Come on, God! Do it for me! I don't ask for much. Do you hear me, God!

I didn't realize that I was praying out loud until the others were embracing me and crying at the same time.

All we could do was wait.

And that was what we did.

Wait.

Chapter 1

Keith

It was a breezy Monday morning, and I hustled into work with the stride of a cheetah. Not because I was anxious to get to work, but because I was running late once again. I had a hangover that was giving me the business right now. I had on my shades to mask the contempt I had for having to work hard after a night of partying hard.

"Keith," I heard a voice call out as I swiftly passed an office. It was a familiar voice. One I chose to ignore at the present time. I did not have any time at all to be an actor.

The person to whom this voice belonged decided to follow me. I entered my office and closed the door behind me. That did not deter the person from entering.

"Are you okay?" The feminine voice made me cringe. I did not hate this person. I just needed time to get myself together. Like until the end of the day.

"Why would you ask that?" I asked as I eased down onto the butter-soft leather chair I had behind my desk.

"Because you were walking like you had to use the bathroom," she said and then chuckled. I did not find it funny.

Jennifer was a loan officer with the bank. I was a senior loan officer. She thought that we were equals. Maybe because she did anything I asked of her. Jennifer was very pleasant to be around, and she made my days at work easier. She was just a bit too bubbly for this early in the morning. Most mornings. I wasn't in a hungover state every day, but on many Mondays my senses were impaired from a night of relaxation and inebriation.

"That was not the issue," I said as I took off my sunglasses and sat them on my desk. "I just have some things to work on, and I am behind." I looked her in the eyes and smiled.

"Okay. You just had me worried. That's all."

"I thank you for your concern. Now let me get myself together, and I will get with you shortly."

"Humph. That was a tad bit sharp." She glared at me, then headed to the door. She could be sensitive at times. Or perhaps I was being sharp. It was a toss-up.

"Nope, this is . . . Close the door behind you." I laughed, and so did she as she exited my office. That was our relationship. Give and take.

I got up from my chair and walked around my desk. I had pictures of my family and friends on my desk and on a bookcase on one side of the room. I looked back at the name plate on my desk. It read KEITH ADAMS, SENIOR LOAN OFFICER. I was proud of my title, but I wanted more. Promotions were not being handed out at the rate I would have liked. I wanted to be further ahead than I was right now. I was not lazy, and I had worked my way into this office. It just seemed like I was standing still.

Money management was my greatest skill. I had inherited it from my parents, who had adopted me when I was fourteen. They were great stewards of money, and they had made sure that I was well versed in handling money too. I lived to make them proud and myself wealthy. I had been on the right track, but, again, everything had stalled. And now I was questioning myself. I needed to do something to speed up this process.

Chapter 2

Justin

I looked at myself in the mirror. I liked what I saw. I was a handsome man. I was proud of my accomplishments.

Growing up in Baltimore had been very interesting. With its gun violence, its corrupt politicians, and a menacing squeegee boy problem, this city had got a bad rep. All you heard about when I was a kid was murder and crime. You would have thought that people were getting murdered around the clock. But that was not true. But the homicide rate was highlighted on the evening news and in the papers.

Even though life in Baltimore was not as bad as the media portrayed it, my childhood was hardly ideal. Both of my parents died from a drug overdose. And plenty of people met the same end in Baltimore in those days. But I vowed early on that I wasn't going to be a statistic or make excuses. I decided to use my parents' demise as a reason to keep going. And, even better, I was going to succeed in life. I didn't want to be coddled. I didn't want special privileges. I matured at a young age and pulled myself up by my own bootstraps. Now I was reaping the rewards of my hard work. I was part of the good news about Baltimore.

After my parents died, one right after the other, I was put in the system, and I survived that experience with the help of my friends Marcus, Keith, and Evan. Was it easy? No, but I didn't let anything stop me from becoming the man that I was today. To combat some of the bad influences in my surroundings, I had made sure to frequent Baltimore's museums and historic landmarks when I was a teenager. And I visited the city's different cultural areas, like Little Italy and the Amish markets, and sampled the food. Sometimes I would just pick a restaurant that normally I would not try. I wanted to remain open-minded and to counter any negative images that I had in my mind.

Nowadays, I walked out of my home with my head held high on most days. Today was one of those days. I hopped in my car, pulled off, and headed toward my first client of the day at the rehab center where I worked.

"Come on, Mr. Alan. You can do it," I said as I helped my patient out of the bed. This forty-year-old Latino guy had had a stroke and was now in rehab. I cared for him in between his therapy sessions. He was a big guy and needed to lose weight. Caring for patients in rehab was my job, and I loved it. It was a challenge that brought joy to my life.

"You got me?" he questioned.

"I got you, sir," I answered as I helped him get across the room to his commode.

Mr. Alan was a good-looking guy with a few gray hairs sprinkled throughout his short, curly hair. I helped him pull down his shorts so that he could relieve himself, and I could not help but notice how good his manhood looked as he sat down. I tried not to stare too hard, but that sight was pleasing to the eyes, to say the least.

"Thanks for your help, Justin. You are always so gentle with me." He looked at me and smiled. His smile made me horny. I had to snap out of it.

"Just doing my job, sir," I replied and then walked away.

I walked toward the window in his room. Thoughts swam around in my mind, the same ones that consumed me daily. I was lonely. I mean, I had some great friends, but that was all that they were. I wanted a companion to go home to every night, not just a series of one-night stands.

Mr. Alan was eye candy and was good to look at while I helped him recover, but he was a married man. His beautiful wife paid him a visit about every other day. His eyes lit up every time she crossed the threshold of his room.

I would not try anything with him, because I knew that he was a straight man. I was not sure that he knew I was gay. I did not carry myself in a feminine way or in any way that could possibly make him uncomfortable. Don't get it twisted. I was a proud gay man, but I was not a billboard.

"I'm finished," he called out, snapping me out of my daze.

I went back to my duties and got one more peek at the third leg he had between the two others God gave him. A mature man always made me horny. I wanted more than physical pleasure, though. I wanted to be loved on and to love on someone whom I could call my own. And good sex was an added bonus.

I was a patient man, but I needed this love thing to move faster than it had. I was not an old man, but I was about to choose one if a man my age with some sense and positive vibes did not come along soon.

Chapter 3

Marcus

"So, tell me what is going on with you today?" I asked a patient of mine as we sat across the room from each other. She has been my patient for about six months now, and she was getting on my nerves with her problems. Yes, I was a therapist, and I liked the money that I was making, but these days I got tired of listening to other people's problems. I had had my own practice for about six years, and it was quite lucrative, to say the least. I truly had no financial problems. I was just bored.

"Ronald called me again," she said and then sighed.

Ronald was her on again, off again lover, and he used her relentlessly, and she loved it. He borrowed her money and her vagina at will. She was a ho, but I could not tell her that outright. I had wanted to do it on many occasions, but her insurance paid well, so I was going to ride this out since she wanted to be ridden. I was leading this horse to the water, but I was taking the scenic route on purpose.

"And what transpired?" I inquired. I knew what she was going to say, but I would let her lead. I wanted to pull out the tape of our last session so that we could get right to the end of the same story, but I did my job and listened.

"He called me at about ten o clock at night, saying he had an emergency and needed to come over," she explained with a sunken look on her face.

She looked sad, but I knew that she loved being dogged out by this man. She had shown me a picture of him once, and he was a very good-looking guy. He was a bum, nonetheless.

"Okay?" I said, prodding so she would continue.

"Well, when he got to my apartment, I didn't let him in right away. I partially opened the door so that he didn't assume I was going to let him right in. You know, like you told me to do. Set some boundaries."

"Great job." I smiled. That was one of the directions I had given her a few sessions ago.

"Continue," I said, prodding her again. I wanted to get this twenty minutes over with.

"Well, he pulled it out right there in the hallway as we talked." Her eyes lit up as she talked.

"Really?" I sat up, as this did pique my interest.

"Yes, he waved like it was the American flag at a baseball game." She was really smiling now. "Then I got weak." Her head dropped, and I saw tears fall.

I got weak too. I felt for her.

"Before I knew it, he had me bent over the couch, enjoying orgasm after orgasm."

My manhood hardened as I thought about her passion. I almost forgot that I was in a session with her and not him. My imagination took me to exotic places many times during these sessions.

"How was it?" I mistakenly asked.

"Huh?" She looked at me in confusion.

"I mean, what happened next?" I shifted in my seat, trying to mask my embarrassment.

"He asked to borrow some money." She looked away in shame.

My eyebrows rose in my effort to act shocked. "And?"

"He said he needed to pay some bills, so I loaned him some money."

"A loan is something you get back, maybe with interest." I paused to give her time to mull this over. "Has he paid you back from the last time?" I asked. I knew the answer, but I let her say it.

"No, but he said that he was in love with me." She smiled as she looked at me. I wanted to smack some sense into her.

"Where do they cash in love?" I asked.

"Huh?" She looked confused.

"Rebecca, do you really think that he loves you?"

"Yes. He tells me all the time," she said, but there was no confidence in her voice. "You don't think he loves me?" She looked at me, searching for the hope that I did not have.

"You, no, but parts of you are readily available to him. You do not see the problem with that?" I said.

"He can learn to love the rest of me, and I him. That's love, right?"

"Your version." I looked at her, hoping she would get it.

"I like my version," she asserted, refusing to be disillusioned with her relationship. She really believed in herself. She was going to be a patient of mine for a long time. But she was not alone in her naivete. I had patients confronting different scenarios who also believe their own hype. I got paid to help them through their problems. Some were easier to enlighten than others.

After I had sessions with three more people that day, I was exhausted. I could not wait to go out to the club for a few hours and hang with my boys. It was always a great way to escape the lives of the people I counseled and my own life. I could feel the liquid calm even before I got there.

Chapter 4

Evan

Evan was my name, and getting people into shape was my game. I loved the intensity of getting people to see the necessity of being in top form. Health care and self-care were both mental and physical. My work provided a high for me. Seeing a person change right in front of my eyes was a miracle to me.

The problem that I had was that some of my clients turned me on, and sometimes we crossed the line. This didn't happen with everyone, of course, but it happened often enough. You see, I was considered the best-looking one in my group of friends. I had a light caramel complexion and tight, curly hair. I had a smile that showed my pretty white teeth. I wasn't on any conceited business, but I got plenty of attention. None of my friends would be considered ugly by a long shot. In fact, we were all good looking. But I was in better shape than any of them, and that got me tons of attention. And I dressed to get attention too. Almost everything that I bought fit my body perfectly.

Many of my clients came from the clubs that I frequented with my friends. I trained men and women, but mainly men. I threw a few women in the mix to attract more money. I was cute, and the women wanted me. I would string them along sometimes to keep that money flowing. It sounded mean, but the women and I got what we all wanted in the end.

I had a dude in front of me right now who was doing a couple of reps of push-ups. He had been training with me for a month or two now. I was feeling him, and I was crotch watching, as he hadn't put spandex on underneath his shorts like normal men did to keep their manhood in place. I watched it flop up and down like a limp fish.

I was getting paid well to train this brother, but I wanted to train in other ways. I was horny beyond belief. It seemed like I always wanted to get it in. It was said that men thought about sex constantly, and I agreed wholeheartedly.

"Hey, good job, Allen," I said. He got up off the floor. He was a dark-skinned guy, and that turned me on as well. I loved dark-skinned men. He looked to be in his midtwenties.

"You think so?" he asked. His breathing was labored, but that was natural. He had sweat all over his body. He reached for one of the exercise machines and grabbed the towel that he had hanging over it.

"Dude, you are getting it in." I patted him on the stomach.

"It just doesn't seem like I am getting the results I want." He looked deflated.

"Listen, stop rushing things, and let me worry about your progress," I told him.

"Okay." A smile crept across his face. It made me weak in the knees.

"Now do some reps of jumping jacks," I ordered.

He started to do what I had asked. I watched the show and enjoyed every moment of it. My imagination was going crazy as I watched his manhood flop around.

The thing was, I didn't know if he was gay or not. Or if he knew that I was. He was a referral from one of the women I was training.

After about another hour of working out, we both headed to the showers. The health club that I trained at had a common shower area and a few private stalls. We both headed to the common area with towels on.

"Thanks for doing all that you do for me. I appreciate it," he said as he took off his towel and stepped in front of a showerhead. I was supposed to be looking at his face, but his soft manhood got most of my attention.

I took my towel off and did the same thing that he had done. We both took a shower and talked about random things.

"So, what does your girl think about your progress?" I asked, probing.

"That's not my speed, if you know what I mean."

"I'm confused," I said, playing dumb.

"I like men," he said in a hushed tone. Like he didn't want anyone to hear him. I played along.

"Don't worry. Your secret is safe with me," I assured him.

"I appreciate that. You still must be careful these days, even though being gay is more acceptable now."

"True." I nodded in agreement.

"You cool with that too, right?"

"No judgment over here."

"At first, I worried, since you're a straight guy training a gay guy. I was nervous about it making you uncomfortable."

I was a proud gay guy, but I didn't give off that vibe to many people. It was what it was. Whether you picked up on it or not, I was cool with it. It did have its advantages, and I used them most of the time.

We both dried off and proceeded to get dressed.

"Hey, did you want to go grab a smoothie really quick?" he asked. "If not, it's okay. I just wanted to thank you for being so encouraging about my training. I don't want you to think that I'm coming on to you."

"That never crossed my mind," I lied to him. I was horny after that shower, and it took everything in me not to advance my plan to explore his body. "I would love to."

We made our way to Tropical Smoothie Café and grabbed some smoothies. It was a few blocks down the street, so the drive there was short. There was silence in the car as I drove. I did not know what to say to him. In my mind, we were just trainer and client.

I pulled up to the shop, and we exited the car and walked in. Tropical Smoothie Café was usually busy at this time of the day, but today that wasn't the case. We both ordered a smoothie and a flatbread sandwich. Then we waited off to the side as our order was being prepared.

"I just love their food here. It is almost always fresh," he remarked.

"That is true," I replied. I tried to focus on him, but my eyes wandered. He was attractive, but I had a short attention span. I wanted to be alone.

Before long, the food prep guy called out our order, giving me a sense of relief. We left the establishment and hopped back in my car.

Before I could start up the car, Allen asked me a question.

"Do you mind taking me home? My car is in the shop. If you can't, I have no problem with doing an Uber." He looked at me with a slight frown.

"Sure. Just give me your address so that I can get the directions."

He did as I had requested, and I pulled off in the direction I was given by the GPS.

I drank my smoothie as I drove and was finished by the time I got to his house. That was typical for me and their smoothies. I loved them.

When we arrived at his home, he proceeded to get out of my car.

"Hey, can I use your bathroom quick?" I said as I leaned over to catch his eye. "I don't know what happened with that smoothie, but I must relieve myself. I am not going to make it home in time. Besides, I hate driving and have the urge to go to the bathroom while in traffic. That is pure torture."

He nodded. "No problem. I totally understand."

Everything in me was leaping with excitement. I knew what I was doing was wrong, but it was what it was.

We entered his apartment, and he directed me to the bathroom. I admired the light masculine décor of his apartment as I did my business and exited the bathroom.

I headed toward the front door, but midway I paused to comment on his apartment. "Nice place, sir," I said. "You have excellent taste."

"Thank you," he said with a smile.

"All right. Thanks for letting me use the bathroom. I'll be on my way."

"You don't have to run out so fast." He laughed. "I hope me being gay doesn't makes you feel uncomfortable. People say they are comfortable with gay people, but they lie to save face. I'm cool with that."

"That's not me at all," I replied. "I'm not a homophobe or anything like that."

"Really?" he asked.

"Nope," I answered. "In fact, I'm gay too."

"You are?" He looked surprised. "I don't believe you. Are you just saying that to make me feel at ease?"

"I am too old to play those games."

"Okay," he said and smiled. "I'm glad because I have a serious crush on you, and I was hoping I didn't do anything that would run you off, because you are such a great trainer."

"I'm flattered." I smiled.

"Would you like something a bit more adult to drink?" he asked. "That smoothie was great, but I need an alcoholic drink."

I was not one to turn down a drink, and I felt the same way that he did.

It didn't take anything more than a drink or two before he was on his knees in front of me, giving me the pleasure of my life. I returned the favor and then exited his place with a buzz and a sexual healing, as they said. I went home and chilled for a bit before I headed out to the club to hang with my boys.

Chapter 5

Keith

We were in our element. The club we were at to-night was lit. I loved hanging out with my boys. We had a table next to one of the walls. The Weeknd was playing, and we had drinks in our hands. This was love. This was life. This was us.

"Evan, why you look so happy?" I asked.

"I'm always happy," he replied. He was right, for the most part. He looked good in his outfit, which hugged his every muscle. I was a bit jealous of his form, but I loved food too much to be about that fit life. I might change my mind, but that would happen later.

"You look like you got some action," Marcus chimed in.

"Maybe," Evan smirked.

"He sure does." Justin laughed.

"I hope it wasn't with one of your clients again," Marcus commented.

"It wasn't my fault this time. He came on to me. I was just a willing and innocent participant." Evan smiled.

"No, you were horny, and he fell in your lap," I retorted.

"He didn't fall, baby. He had his kneepads ready." Evan laughed.

"You should be ashamed of yourself," Marcus said, chastising him. "Pooping where you work is a no-no in my book."

"I couldn't help myself," Evan said before he took a sip of his drink. "He was a hot boy with a hot toy, and I pressed PLAY on that joystick."

We all laughed at Evan's last comment because we were all guilty of weak moments of passion.

"At least you are getting some," Justin said.

"It's not my fault you haven't met the man of your dreams. You work too much at cleaning up old people. You need to participate in some self-care, if you know what I mean," Evan quipped.

"I don't date people where I work. And the people at work need me," Justin responded and then finished off his drink.

"Good for you, Justin," Marcus told Justin. "Your man will come along. Take your time."

"I agree," I added. "But a quickie does sound good right about now."

It had been a minute for me as well. Being focused on my career and getting ahead had dulled my love life.

"Keith, it has been a minute for you. Why is that?" Evan said.

"I'm just focusing on my career right now. I want to have certain things in place before I get back onto the dating scene," I informed him.

"So how is that coming along?" Marcus asked.

"I'm feeling like I have stalled," I answered. "It's so frustrating." I drank the last of my drink. I was beginning to feel the buzz, but I knew I needed to grab another to ease my depression.

"I feel you on that," Marcus commented. "I feel the same way. I'm tired of listening to people's problems. The money is good, but I need some adventure. I'm bored to tears" he confessed.

"Y'all need a nice, stiff—"

"Evan, sex is not always the answer," I interrupted.

"I didn't say it was the answer. I said y'all need some. A little dab will do ya." He laughed.

We couldn't help but laugh, because he was serious and partially correct. I was in a drought in that area.

"I don't need any reminders, but I damn sure need another drink," I announced.

My boys all agreed and ordered more drinks to get us through our problems.

As the night wore on, we drank more, talked some more, and danced a little bit. This was another hangover waiting to happen.

Chapter 6

Justin

We had a great time, as usual, at the club tonight. Drinking and laughter did help with the problems of life. At least at that moment.

After I left the club, I hopped in my car and drove only a block before I pulled over and turned off the ignition. I just sat there and thought about my life and about going home to an empty house again. The thought of the empty house awaiting me began to kill the fresh buzz I currently had. I picked up my phone and browsed for a few minutes on social media. It seemed that everyone was living their best life except me. I knew that this wasn't true, but I was in my feelings. I threw my phone onto the passenger seat and then hung my head a bit. Depression sucked big-time.

A knock on my front passenger window pulled me out of my stupor.

I looked over at the person who was bent over, looking at me. He was a good-looking guy. I hesitantly rolled down my window a bit.

"You all right?" he asked.

"I'm good," I replied. I already had the car on and my gearshift in drive. I was drunk, but I was not a fool. It was close to one thirty in the morning. I believed that freaks came out at night. Freaks, murderers, and plenty of weirdos.

He must have noticed that I was ready to drive off. "I'm not a killer. I promise. Just a concerned citizen." He smiled. He had some beautiful teeth and eyes.

"I appreciate the thought. But I'm good, though." I rolled up my window to signal to him that I was finished with him.

He tapped on my window again. I lowered it again.

"You lost?" I asked.

"No. I'm where I want to be." He smiled again.

"You sure?"

"Yes. I noticed you in the club, and I was feeling you. But I didn't want to approach you with your friends around. It looked like you all were having a good time. I just wanted to know if I could get your number or if I could give you mine. I'm not on no stalker-type stuff. I'm just interested in getting to know you. Maybe more."

"Are you drunk?" I asked.

"I got a buzz, but I'm clear about my attraction to you."

It has been a few months since I had had someone other than clients and bill collectors interested in me. I must admit that he had piqued my interest.

"So, who am I talking to?" I asked. I looked around to take note of my surroundings just in case this was a setup. Truth be told, I was not street savvy, as they said, and I probably would have been assaulted by now if something was wrong.

"I'm Marlon," he said and reached his arm through the open window to shake my hand.

"I'm Justin," I replied as I thrust my hand toward his. Our hands met, and I discovered that his was strong yet soft, and I melted on the inside. I hated beginnings. I was as vulnerable as a kitten in front of a pit bull.

"Justin, that is a great smile you have."

"What smile?" I involuntarily smiled. I could have slapped myself for being so foolish.

"That one," he pointed out. "So, are you going to give me the digits, or do I have to go home broken-hearted?" He put on a fake frown, which convinced me to fulfill his request. He had my attention.

I gave him my number, and he put it in his phone. I said my goodbye, and I pulled off toward home.

It didn't take long for him to send me a text message.

This is Marlon. Text me back if you believe in love at first sight.

I was speechless. I pulled up to my house about twenty minutes later. I showered, grabbed a snack, and then lay across my bed.

My phone lay beside me, face down, as I munched on a peanut butter and jelly sandwich. My heart and mind were racing. I picked up my phone and replied to his text.

I'm a believer.

Shortly after I sent the text, I fell into a deep sleep. I woke up the next morning with my head spinning from the night before. I had done too much drinking and had had too much fun, and now I was paying for it.

I slowly got dressed. Then Marlon and I texted for about a half hour before I let him know that I had to be at work in a few hours.

As I drove to the rehab center later that morning, I had to admit that I was curious and skeptical about Marlon at the same time. I just hoped that I wasn't wasting my time. Love had just been too damn elusive for me to trust that it was knocking at my window.

Chapter 7

Marcus

I breathed a sigh of relief as my last patient left my office for the day. I was glad that I could make my own schedule. It was one of the luxuries of having your own business. I packed up my briefcase so I could make some notes tonight.

I had decided that today would be devoted in part to some self-care, and that included taking myself out to lunch. I was hungry, but I was a cheap date, so I ended up at Outback Steakhouse. It was one of the places l loved to go to when I was alone.

I arrived at the establishment and was seated in a booth within ten minutes of walking through the door. Once I sat down, a server appeared, and I asked for a glass of water with a slice of lemon. Minutes later he delivered the water and complimentary brown bread.

I was browsing the menu when I heard a voice that I recognized all too well. My eyes lit up as I watched a giddy and bubbly patient of mine being seated with a guy who I assumed was her moocher. I had to admit that he was a very good-looking guy. Their table had a fine view of mine, so I scooted into a corner of the booth so as not to be seen. I was hoping that she didn't spot me, since I hated socializing with the people I treated. I wasn't better than them. It was just that they usually wanted free sessions on the fly. I needed my coin for every problem I talked a patient through. No freebies at all.

I picked my menu up and hid my face, trying not to be obvious.

"I knew that looked like you over here," she said as she walked over to my table.

I cringed at the thought of having been spotted, and now I had to put on the phony act of being human and social.

"Let me introduce you to Ronald." She motioned for me to follow her.

I hesitantly left my booth. I walked behind her to the table where they were seated.

"Ronald, this is Marcus. He's—" she began, getting right to the introductions, but I cut her off.

"A high school friend," I said, and then I smiled as I looked at her. He didn't need to know who I really was to her and I didn't want him to know. I hoped she was not discussing our sessions with him. That would be just dumb.

Ronald looked up for a split second before he went back to staring at his menu. "Cool. I'm ready to eat," he mumbled.

I was embarrassed for her, but I didn't let it show. I just smiled the whole time, waiting for the right moment to make my escape.

Their waitress came over to the table, giving me the perfect excuse to part ways with them.

"Enjoy your food," I said as I turned on my heel and walked away.

I got back to my booth and sighed in relief. Once I had gathered myself, a picture of Ronald popped into my head, and stories she had told me about him swirled around my mind. A face and body to match the stories made me unexpectedly horny.

The urge to use the bathroom hit me just as my server came back to take my order.

"Before you take my order, I need to use the men's room," I said, getting out of my booth.

"I will get your order when you come back."

I passed the table my client was sitting at on my way to the bathroom. I didn't even acknowledge them as I walked by.

Once inside the bathroom, I headed to one of the urinals and relieved myself. It was a relief, as usual.

As soon as I turned to go to the sink and wash my hands, I bumped into Ronald. He was a tall,

well-built dark chocolate man. I caught a whiff
of his scent and then backed up. My manhood
awakened.

"My bad," I said as I walked around him and
toward the sink.

"No problem," he said as continued to the urinals.

I watched him relieve himself through the mirror that was opposite the urinals. He then turned
around and waved his manhood at me. I was
caught in a slight trance for a few seconds.

"You like what you see?" he said as he made his
way toward me.

I was speechless. The thought of him being this
bold in a public bathroom turned me all the way
on.

"Huh?" I answered.

He put himself away as he walked toward the
sink. "I'm not even hard." He grabbed my hand
and rubbed it on his crotch.

"Damn," I muttered in a low tone. I looked up
at him, and he smiled. I forgot where I was for a
moment.

"I know, right?" He chuckled. He was cocky. But
he was fine too. Too damn fine. Fine and broke.

"I need to go," I said as I backed away from him.

"Don't run. I play on both sides of the fence."
He laughed. "I'd love some playtime with you. No
strings. Just fun."

He closed in on me as I reached the door. He
put his arm on the door, blocking me in. Then he

leaned toward me and sniffed my neck. His hot breath made me lose all my morals for a second.

He rattled off his phone number and then backed away. I moved away from the door.

"Put it in your phone and text me when you are ready to play," he said in his deep voice. It sounded like an order.

He exited the bathroom a moment later, and against all the wisdom I had accrued, I took out my phone and saved his number under the name Playmate.

Finally, I left the bathroom, walked back to my table, and didn't even glance in their direction.

I sat down in my booth and picked up my menu and tried to find something to eat. But what I wanted wasn't on the menu. I settled on a few appetizers, and after consuming them, I left the restaurant and went home.

Despite feeling distracted, I managed to spend a few hours making notes on my patients, but when ten o'clock rolled around, I called it a night. I rolled around in my bed for over an hour, fighting the urge to text Ronald. But when the scene in the bathroom popped into my head, I grabbed my phone to send out a text.

It read I want some playtime.

I rolled over and went to sleep, hoping that this decision didn't come back to bite me.

Chapter 8

Evan

I was in the middle of training a young lady who was trying to get her baby weight off. These were my favorite clients, because they were serious about returning to form. Especially the married ones. She was married to a real estate investor, and she was not trying to lose her man to anyone. I didn't blame her. I saw a picture of them together when she showed me what she had looked like before the baby. He was a great-looking Asian and could sell me some property anytime. If you know what I mean.

"Susan, you are really coming along," I complimented her. It was partially true. Egging on my clients was a part of the business. I had to keep them coming back.

"Really?" she asked.

"I don't waste my breath or my time. I specialize in results, and you are coming along great."

"Evan, if I wasn't already married, I would be all over you." She laughed.

I wanted to tell her that she was shaking the wrong tree, but I kept my true thoughts in my head. I need referrals, which brought me more money. A little white lie had never hurt anyone.

Susan was my last client for the day. I was just ready to go home and take a break and then head to the club with my boys tonight.

Once my session with Susan had ended, I packed up my things and exited the gym. I could almost taste the alcohol now, long before I even got to the club. I walked to my car with a smile on my face, only to be surprised to find a person standing by my car. It was Allen.

"Hey, Evan," he greeted me as I got to my car.

"Hey, Allen." I kept the smile on my face. "How are you? Is everything okay?" I asked, because the last time I saw him was when we hooked up. He didn't have an appointment until later this week.

"Yes." He smiled back. "I just wanted to say hi."

"Oh, that is sweet," I said as I unlocked my car door. I got in the car and put my seat belt on. Allen leaned on my car, right near the open driver's door.

"Did you need a ride somewhere?" I asked, looking up at him. He seemed like the shy type when it came to interacting with people. He wasn't a bad-looking dude.

"Yeah, my car is still down, and I was in the area." He made his way around the car and hopped into the passenger seat. "I hope it's not an inconvenience for you."

"No problem. It's on my way," I said as I backed out of my parking spot. I headed in the direction of his house.

It took about twenty minutes to get to his house. I parked in the parking spot in front of his door and waited for him to exit the car.

"Can you come up again today? You know, to talk?" he asked as he unbuckled his seat belt.

I knew what he meant, and I was flattered, but I had to turn him down. I was tired, and I just wanted to get a nap in before hitting the club tonight.

"Well, I can't, because I have some plans with some friends tonight. Maybe another time," I said with a sad face.

"It will only take a half hour or less. I promise." He smiled.

I was weak. I placed the car in park, turned off the ignition, and then made my way into his house with him.

He was right. It was a quick session. We went a little further than the last time. I was sure to use protection, which he had a good supply of.

"Thanks for coming up," he said as he lay next to me on his couch. He had a big smile on his face as I turned and looked at him.

"Thanks for the invite. It was worth it," I said as I sat up.

"You can wash up in the bathroom. There are some washcloths on the sink."

I got up and cleaned myself up quickly and made my way to the door. I was tired now and had performed well in a short period of time.

"Thanks for the good time. I will see you later this week. Rest up," I said. Then I exited his home without even waiting for a response.

When I got home, I showered and crashed in my bed for a few hours. Then I hopped up, got dressed, and headed out to the club to meet up with my boys.

Chapter 9

Keith

It was another day at the office. Client after client came in, and I handled my business as usual. Every client I dealt with as a loan officer at the bank had a unique set of personal problems, which they were quick to share. Problems such as cheating mates, Mommy or Daddy issues, an inability to get along with siblings, compulsive disorders, and more depression than I cared to talk about. Hearing about these problems didn't make my job easier. And I still felt stagnant when it came to moving up the corporate ladder. I put in long hours, and I was still in the same spot.

After all the work I had put in by midday, I was tired. I was tired and depressed.

"You look beat," Jennifer stated as she peeked into my office through the slightly open door.

"Well, that is an understatement," I said as I got up from my desk chair. I stretched and then sat back down in my chair and slouched down.

It was 1:30 p.m., and it seemed and felt like I had been at work for much longer.

"I got some news for you," she revealed as she walked into my office. She sat down in the chair on the other side of my desk and leaned in.

"What?" I sat up straight.

"Wow. You are an eager beaver, aren't you?" She laughed.

"You're not a comedienne, so spill it," I responded.

"We have a new boss, and he is coming in today," she said in a hushed tone. "And, baby, he is fine as wine." She smiled with glee.

I was curious as to how she knew this and I didn't.

"How did you find this out?" I asked.

"Well, I got my sources." She had a smug look on her face.

"I bet," I responded, throwing out what might be construed as a petty insult by someone who didn't know how Jennifer and I bantered with each other. It was all in fun.

"His name is Kingston Clark," she revealed. "Doesn't that name sound sexy and exotic?"

"Well, haven't seen an ugly Kingston before." I nodded my head. My imagination was in overdrive now, and the thoughts swirling in my head made me even more curious about the new boss.

"What time is he supposed to be here?" I asked.

"I don't know, but I am ready and willing to perform at maximum capacity. If you know what I mean." She giggled.

"Now, you know that it's not professional to try to sleep with your boss."

"That's why you are where you are right now. A few back strokes from the boss never hurt nobody." She burst into a fit of laughter.

"Integrity and ethics are the keys to getting promoted, not laying on your back," I smirked.

"I don't work on my back, but my knees are oiled and ready to serve the needy. These days the only way up is to go down."

I shouldn't have laughed, but I did.

Just then, there was a knock on the door, which interrupted our chat.

"Come in," I called out.

It was one of the customer service representatives. "We have a visitor. He is handsome and looks important."

"Okay. I will be out in a second," I said.

"It's him," Jennifer said before she hopped out of her chair and dashed out of my office. I guessed she wanted a head start, but it was no contest. I was a professional, and I would let my work speak for me.

I spruced up my office a bit and then made my way out into the hallway. I was a bit nervous, to say the least. I headed to the lobby area, where a few people had surrounded the new guy. From the looks of it, Jennifer had magically lost a button on her already tight blouse, as one of her breasts was almost popping out now.

The closer I got to the new boss, the more I realized that this guy was living up to the name his parents had given him. He wasn't drop-dead gorgeous, but he did turn heads. In other words, he was easy on the eyes.

"You must be Keith," he said after I'd edged into the circle of people around him. He reached out to shake my hand, and I returned the gesture. It seemed like he shook my hand a bit longer than one normally would. But that could be my imagination.

"Yes, I am he," I said and smiled, keeping it professional.

"I am so glad to be working with you all to make this place an even more well-oiled machine," he commented, addressing all of us.

We all nodded our heads in agreement. The way he spoke commanded attention but not in an aggressive way. He talked with confidence and made eye contact. It made me feel at ease. I was glad that he was not cocky or arrogant. At least, that was not what I felt from him presently.

He went on. "I will be speaking to each of you individually in order to relay to you my expectations. I will be starting with you, Keith."

"Yes, sir," I answered.

"No sirs around here. My name is Kingston. Please greet me as such."

We all nodded our heads in agreement.

Ten minutes later, after the impromptu meeting in the lobby had broken up, he followed me back to my office, where he and I sat down across from each other.

"Keith, I have read up on you, and I am very happy with the numbers I see from you."

"I love what I do." I smiled with pride. "I love my job."

"The numbers show it," he told me. "So where do you see yourself going with this company?"

"I want to go up as far as I can," I answered, speaking with confidence. "I was made for this. I live and breathe this." I sounded like a commercial, but I meant every word I said.

"That is what I like to hear." He smiled. "I am going to take you out to dinner so that we can get better acquainted. I want to hear all the ideas that you have to push us into the stratosphere."

"Dinner?" I asked.

"Yes, I like to eat, talk, and get to know the people I work with individually. Is that a problem?"

"No, it's that I have never been asked to dinner by a supervisor before. Well, not at this job."

"Well, I'm all about newness and personal relationships with my workers. My motto is 'People don't care what you know until they know what you are.'"

"That is an excellent statement. And I agree with it wholeheartedly."

He stood suddenly and exited my office as quickly as he'd come in. I was excited and nervous at the same time. What kind of boss took his workers out for dinner to get to know them? My new boss, that was who.

Chapter 10

Justin

I have some great friends, I thought as I lay back on the balcony to my apartment. The cool Baltimore breeze had picked up because it was late in the day. I had my feet up and a mimosa sitting next to me. I was an avid reader, and I had book that I was reading called *Both Sides of the Fence*, by this guy named M.T. Pope. It was a pretty good read. Anyway, I loved these moments alone, as well as the time I spent with my boys at the club.

Keith, Evan, Marcus, and I had been through some tough times in life. We were connected through cloudy pasts. What were the odds of four inner-city guys meeting in a group home? And add to that the fact that we were all gay. Unbelievable but true. We had all bounced around from group home to group home until we all met and bonded at the last one.

I remembered it like it was yesterday.

I walked with a nervous rumble in my stomach. It wasn't a new experience for me, just a new place. Newness had always scared me. I was so glad that my representative, a social worker, was right beside me as I walked into this new group home. I was nervous because I was hoping that me being gay didn't get exposed right away.

Every group home I had been in thus far was almost always full of straight boys, who tried to prove how masculine they were by trying to beat the gay out of me. I was not overly feminine, but I didn't mask my gayness either. I tried to mind my business most of the time. I just wanted to be friendly and outgoing.

"Hey, everyone. This is Justin. He will be joining you," my representative announced to the group of boys who had assembled to meet me.

I tried to be brave and to look all the boys in the eye as they gazed at me with curiosity in their eyes. There were some cute faces in the mix of brown-skinned boys. This made me feel a bit better. Eye candy was always good, even if these boys were potentially jerks and bullies.

I put my book bag and suitcase down on the floor in order to finalize the agreement I had with my new home. After I signed a few papers, the lady in charge offered to show me around.

"Come. Let me show you the room you will be staying in," she said as she put her hand on my shoulder. I looked at my representative, and she nodded her head in agreement. She then turned around and walked out the door.

I followed behind my new parental figure, my book bag over my shoulder and my suitcase in hand, as she walked up a long flight of stairs and then headed down a hallway toward a huge bedroom. There were four twin beds that had been strategically placed in the room, so that each boy had his own space. One bed and one dresser for each. The room was clean, for the most part. There was just one messy bed.

"You will be sharing this room with Keith, Marcus, and Evan. I think you guys will get along great." She smiled at me, and her smile was filled with hope and confidence. I smiled back, but I had plenty of doubt from my previous experiences in group homes.

"Take your time putting your stuff away. Dinner is in about an hour. I hope you like Salisbury steak, mashed potatoes, and corn." She smiled again.

"Yes, I do." I smiled genuinely and then turned to the bed that I assumed was mine, because the dresser nearby had nothing on it, unlike the others.

As I was unloading my stuff and filling the dresser with my clothes, the room filled up with all the boys, who numbered about eight. I turned to see all of them looking at me like I was a weird science project.

"So, Justin, where are you from?" a tall dude asked. His size was intimidating, to say the least.

"Baltimore," I said with too much sass. Sometimes I got smart without meaning to.

"I mean, what part of Baltimore?" He stepped closer to me. I recoiled a bit, ready to swing at him if I had to swing.

"Park Heights," I answered.

"So, I take it you can fight. Park Heights is a rough area, so I know you can fight."

"Well . . ." I hesitated because I didn't like where it looked like this was going. It looked like this was going to be some type of cage match, and I was the newest arrival. I was no gladiator.

"Don't clam up now," the tall one said. "Throw a few punches so I can see if you're really a brawler."

"A brawler?" I asked. "Nah, that's not me."

"You meaning to tell me that you from Park Heights and you choose not to give us a showcase?"

"I am not a sideshow. I fight only when I must fight." I looked at him and the other boys. I knew how to fight, but it took a lot to get me to that place.

"Wallace, leave him alone," said a deep voice that came from near the door to the room.

I looked over at the door. A large black man stood there. He looked like a figure of authority. I breathed a sigh of relief.

"Y'all go wash up for dinner," the man ordered.

All the boys exited the room, and the big guy walked over to me. I sat down on the bed, and so did he.

"Justin, I am sorry about that. Wallace thinks that he is in charge around here." A light laugh escaped his lips.

It eased my tension instantly.

"The truth is my wife is in charge, and if you don't get cleaned up, there will be hell to pay." He laughed again. I laughed as well. "Get cleaned up and come downstairs to eat."

"Yes, sir." I nodded my head in agreement.

He got up and walked over to the door. He turned around and said, "My name is Mr. Wilson. Welcome home and to the team."

"Thanks." It felt good inside to feel welcomed.

I slowly walked down the stairs and heard noises, which led me to the kitchen. There was a table that was big enough for everyone, plus a few more. There was an empty seat next to Mr. Wilson. I felt that this seat had purposely been left empty for me so that I would feel more comfortable. This couple were good at their jobs.

"Welcome to dinner, Justin," Mr. Wilson said as he waved his hand over the food like he was a game show host revealing a prize. "My wife, Connie, is going to bless the food, and then we will eat."

I nodded my head and then waited for the prayer.

She prayed, and then they methodically served the food, and there was plenty to eat. As I expected, the food was a hit, and everyone was quiet during dinner.

Once all the boys had cleaned their plates, Mr. Wilson stated, "All right, let's get some dessert. And then let's get the showers going."

After dessert, the shower schedule was announced. They had three full bathrooms, which was not unusual for a group home. I got to go first since it was my first time. The grimaces on some of the boys' faces let me know that I was not getting this option all the time.

I showered and then made my way back to the bed to which I was assigned. I tucked myself into bed and pulled the covers over my head so that I could avoid eye contact with the others for as long as possible.

I heard footsteps as each of the boys made their way back to the room. I tried to will myself to fall sleep so that it could be tomorrow already, but that didn't work. I heard every noise in the room as they readied themselves for sleep.

Then silence filled the room. I was under the covers and alone with my thoughts. Then I felt someone sit on my bed. I tensed up. I didn't know what to do. I hoped these boys weren't going to try to rock me to sleep with their fists.

I felt two more people sit down on my bed. I faked a snore so that they would leave me alone and go back to their beds.

It didn't work, because one of them decided to pull the covers off me. I continued to fake sleep.

"He thinks we are falling for this act," I heard one of them say.

"Right. I did the same thing when I was new that he is doing now. Hoping that we will leave him alone," another said, and this was followed by a slight chuckle.

"I guess we are going to have to tickle his feet to see if he is going to come up swinging or laughing."

"I guess so," the third one said, and then they all laughed.

I slowly opened my eyes to all the guys looking directly at me.

"I guess we can't have fun with this one," one of the guys said and then smiled.

"So, which one of us do you like?" the lighter-skinned guy asked.

"What?" I was shocked that he asked me that question. It was totally unexpected.

"Don't play dumb. We know one of our own when we see one."

"I'm lost. What does 'one of our own' mean?" I played dumb for as long as possible. This felt like a setup.

"Ohhh, you want to play *that* game. Maybe I should go get Wallace and see what he has to say about it," the third one said.

"Please don't do that," I said as I sat up in the bed.

"That's means you are going to answer my question," the lighter-skinned one said.

"Truthfully, I'm not attracted to any of you," I said with a straight face.

"But you do admit that you are one of the boys that likes boys," said the third guy.

"Well . . ." I hesitated as I looked at each one of them. They didn't look threatening at all. "Yes." I lowered my head.

"Hey, don't be ashamed," the lighter-skinned one told me. "You are among family. We don't know you, but we already like you. You look like you are low key and chill. We like that."

They all nodded in approval.

I furrowed my brow. "Really?"

"Yes, we stick together, and we don't take no stuff. While we don't advertise our sexuality, we don't play about freedom to be us. We live and let live," said the third guy. "By the way, I am Keith, and this is Evan and Marcus. Stick with us and you will be all right."

Over the next few weeks, our bond got stronger and stronger. We eventually got so close that we felt more like brothers than friends. My life wasn't easy back then, but having these guys in my life made it easier to deal with and manage.

Chapter 11

Marcus

"Damn." I lay back in my bed and breathed out a heavy sigh. I had just finished a phone session with a client of my new playmate. This was how it went.

"Hey, Doc," she said. She called me this sometimes. It annoyed me, but I moved past it. I wanted my patients to feel comfortable talking to me. "I need a session."

"Okay." I noted the time on my phone and pushed RECORD so that I could go back to this session later if need be.

I already knew that this was going to be about Ronald, so I was getting paid to lust over a man who was playing the field and was on both sides of the fence.

"You can start," I said.

"Well, Ronald has been acting funny ever since we left that restaurant we saw you at the other day."

"How so?" I asked.

"He's been paying me more attention than usual."

"Is that a bad thing?" I asked.

"I don't know. I mean, I'm not used to him being affectionate outside of sex."

"Isn't this what you wanted?" I reminded her.

"Yes, but he is going in with it. He's all over me."

"You can't have it both ways, you know. I think you should enjoy it. You wanted this for so long, and now that you have it, you say that it is too much," I replied.

"You are right. I'm acting stupid."

"I wouldn't call it stupid. It's new. You must take the time to get used to it. Progress is work." I wanted to tell her it was too late and I was about to scoop him up, but that would be presumptuous, because I really hadn't done a test run yet. Her comments about him were from her own experience, not mine. And I did want to sample the product for myself. Experience was the best teacher.

"This is why having you on standby is beneficial to my well-being. I love having you in my corner. I know that you are for me and not against me." I could picture her smiling, even though she was on the phone.

I felt bad.

For me to have so much wisdom, it seemed a shame that I wasn't exercising it right now. Yes, I was having second thoughts about this fine man.

But in the final analysis, I wanted to sex him down just to see if she was right about his sexual prowess.

As justification for my actions, I kept telling myself that this was merely an experiment. I wanted to make sure that I counseled her to the fullest. I didn't want to lead her astray. I also was telling myself that she wouldn't know anyway. *What you don't know won't kill you, right*? I thought.

Chapter 12

Evan

The club was jumping tonight. It was the usual. I was looking fine and fly as I sipped on a drink that was getting oh, so right.

I danced in my chair as I watched my friends dance hard on the floor. This was really an escape from the woes of life and decision-making. I continued to bop my head to the latest the Weeknd hit. This was a Friday, and I hadn't scheduled any Saturday appointments. I was going to get my party on tonight. Well, I would just drink. I did not have any rhythm on the dance floor. The only rhythm I needed was in the bedroom, and there was no complaining going on when I got in there. I aimed to please.

A Mary J. song came on, and the crowd on the floor went wild. I did as well, but again from my chair.

"Hey, sir," I heard a voice say behind me. This person was very close to me, causing me to jump.

I turned around to see Allen standing there with a smile on his face.

"Hey," I said, with a slight smile on my face. I was surprised to see him there, but then I remembered that I was in a public place and thought that maybe this was a coincidence that we were here together.

"I'm surprised to see you here," he commented.

"Why is that?" I asked. I wanted to see what his response would be.

"You just don't look like the club type. You come across as sophisticated and refined."

"That is a good answer. I do try to hold myself to a certain standard, but I have a party guy that lives here. Just ignore any craziness that you might see me do in here." I smiled and then took another sip of my drink.

"Are you with someone?" he asked.

"I'm with my friends. They are on the dance floor, so you can sit with me."

He sat down beside me, and we vibed.

"This is my song," he said at one point, and he got up and danced beside his chair. I watched him gyrate and pop his behind to the Christina Aguilera song "Genie in a Bottle." He was getting it in.

He finished dancing when the song ended, and then he hopped back in his chair.

"You got some moves," I told him.

"Thanks." He blushed.

We talked for a few more minutes, and then my boys came back to the table.

"Hey, who is this?" Keith asked as he sat down at the table.

Justin and Marcus waited for an answer as all three of them all stared at Allen and then at me.

"Oh, this is one of my little buddies that I train at the gym. His name is Allen."

"So did you sleep with him?" Marcus asked.

I was dumbfounded for a few seconds. I could not believe that he had asked that in front of everyone. But it wasn't abnormal behavior from the wise guy at the table.

"No, I don't mix business with pleasure," Allen answered for me.

"Wow. So you turned him down?" Marcus asked Allen.

"Are you seriously doing this right now?" I was pissed.

"He's been a perfect gentleman," Allen answered. He looked at me and smiled. I was impressed.

"But you want to get in his pants, though?" Marcus continued.

"I never said that," Allen answered. He sat up straight, and he answered while looking at Marcus in the eyes. He spoke with confidence. He had seemed like a pushover in our talks while working out. I guessed I was wrong.

"Marcus!" Keith yelled to get his attention.

"What?" Marcus looked around like he was doing nothing wrong. "He was the one that said he does not mix business with pleasure. The word *business* said that he liked training him, but the word *pleasure* said that he was ready to get on his knees and give the best that he got. I'm just stating the facts. Words are powerful. Use them wisely."

"I'm sorry, Allen. These are my best friends, most of the time." I smirked as I looked at Marcus.

"Nice to meet you all. I'm going to get going. I'm meeting a friend here. See you next week, Evan," Allen said as he stood.

Chapter 13

Keith

I pulled up to this fancy restaurant, the name of which he had emailed to me. I had to admit that I was nervous, to say the least. I didn't know this guy or what this dinner was all about. I had made sure that I was dressed to impress. I had on some nice shoes, cream slacks, a shirt, and a simple blazer. I sat in my car for a few minutes because I was a half hour early. I believed in punctuality, especially in situations where I was not sure of the agenda. I hoped this was a meet and greet and not a fancy way of firing people. I mean, this would be the perfect setting for me if I were in a position to fire somebody. A professional would not act up in a place like this, but I prayed that this was not my fate today.

I checked myself out in the mirror before I got out of the car. It was a nice breezy fall day, so I took my time as I walked to the door of the restaurant.

"Good evening, sir. May I have the name on your reservation?" the handsome male host said as I walked up to his podium.

"I'm here with Kingston Clark," I answered.

"Oh, Mr. Clark." The host smiled. "He called and said to seat you. He is running behind. And he said to order whatever you wanted."

"Okay. No problem," I said with a faint smile.

The way he smiled back caused me to believe that Kingston was a regular here or something. Or a great tipper.

The host came from behind his podium and proceeded to lead me to the table. Once I was seated, he handed me a menu, and then he rattled off some wines that they had available. I loved good wine, and good free wine was even better. Today would be different, though. I would not be going that route the first time I sat down with my boss.

"I'll take a water with lemon," I said.

"You sure?" he asked.

"Yes. That will be all."

He walked away and shook his head as he went. I just ignored it and looked over the menu to keep my mind occupied as I waited. I didn't know if any of this was a test, but I was aiming to pass.

Fifteen minutes later, Kingston swaggered in. I had to admit that he had it going on. The people in the restaurant were all enamored with him as he walked past their tables.

I stood up and greeted him with a handshake. "Good day, Mr. Clark."

"No formalities today. Just relax and enjoy the evening," he said as he looked me in the eyes. His gaze almost put me in a trancelike state.

He was a good-looking guy. I had thought so the first time I'd met him, and under the restaurant's soft lights, he was looking even better. My lust kicked in, and I had to try to focus on business and not pleasure. That would be hard.

He sat down and looked me in the eyes again.

"I'm so glad that we could meet up. I enjoy getting to know my fellow workers in a neutral setting. Good food and wine help relationships bud and flow without stress. At least, that is what I believe."

I nodded my head in agreement.

"Keith, I hope that you are not intimidated by me. I don't bite on first meetings," he said and then laughed.

"No, sir," I stated. "Just trying to keep it professional."

"I appreciate that, but you can bring it down. This is a 'getting to know you' session. Nothing more. Call me Kingston. Do you have a problem with that?"

"Okay, Kingston," I said with a smile. He was politely aggressive. I loved it. It was a complete turn-on.

"Where are you from?" he asked.

"Right here in Maryland," I answered. "Where are you from?" I asked. It felt freeing to dialogue this way with a superior.

"I was born and raised in Jamaica." His accent flourished when he said the name of his birthplace. He sounded American most of the time. I guessed he could turn it on and off when he wanted. "My family immigrated here when I was four years old. I have six brothers and sisters, who are all educated like myself. What about your family?"

"I am an only child. My parents were killed in a car accident when I was thirteen. I entered the foster care system and went through a few group homes before a nice family adopted me as their own. I have three best friends, whom I met in one of the group homes, and they are my brothers."

"Amazing. So do you have a boyfriend?"

"Excuse me?" I looked at him in shock. It was a totally unexpected question.

"I am a very open-minded person, so please don't be offended by my question."

"I wasn't offended, just shocked."

"Are you avoiding the question?"

"No. I am unattached right now," I answered.

"A handsome guy like you? I am shocked."

I laughed, because I didn't know that you could be uncomfortable and comfortable at the same time. This guy was something else. I didn't know where he was going with this question, but I was intrigued.

"Are you married or single? Gay or straight?" I asked him, to see if he would be honest.

"I'm single and comfortable with myself," he said and then laughed.

"Are you are avoiding the questions too?"

"No. I answered." He smiled. "You didn't like my answer?"

"It was okay. But since you are my boss, I will leave it alone."

"I like you, Keith. I am glad that I get to work with you. I am sure that we are going to achieve great things together. It is my duty to get people to new levels in life. I will do my best to push you higher, if you are willing to put in the work and follow my lead."

"Kingston, I will do whatever you want me to do to go higher."

"People say that but don't really mean it," he said as he looked me in the eyes.

I stared back with confidence. His eyes were piercing my soul. They caused my heart to flutter.

"I'm not like most people. I deliver. My record speaks for itself."

"I work with clean sheets. Your history is while you were working with someone else. I don't know the relationship you had with your other supervisors. I will have to see for myself." He winked at me.

"Well, I deliver results." I smiled. We were still looking at each other sternly. I was not backing down.

"I like your confidence. I feed off confidence." He winked at me again. I then felt his foot on my leg.

I tensed up because I didn't know what to do. Was he flirting with me?

"Oh, I'm sorry. Was that your leg? I thought it was the table leg," he smirked.

"No problem," I said.

The rest of the evening was filled with him sending me mixed messages. One minute it seemed like he was flirting, and the next was like a business conversation. This guy was confusing me.

I rolled with the punches, as the saying went.

When dinner ended, he walked me to my car.

"Thanks for dinner. I will see you at work," I said. I went to open my car door, but he held it closed, which caused me to look at him in confusion.

"I believe in hugs when ending some interactions," he told me.

He was larger than me in stature, but he wasn't a giant. I had an awkward and uneasy feeling about hugging my boss, but I did it anyway.

He pulled me into a tight embrace that had my face pinned to his chest. The aroma of his cologne and the feeling of his tight muscles had me melting on the inside. All my present thoughts were inappropriate in nature. But I loved it all the same. It had been quite some time that I had felt the touch of a man. The embrace lasted for only a few seconds, but it filled my lust bucket completely.

I pulled away and instantly felt shame. How could I be lusting after my new boss? This was not the way I wanted to climb the corporate ladder.

"You smell good. I like that," he said as he looked into my eyes, and then he walked away.

I got in my car, but I could hardly focus on the drive home.

I lay in my bed that night with nothing but lust-filled scenarios running through my head.

Chapter 14

Justin

"Love All Over Me" by Monica flowed through my house as I was cleaning it and doing some daily tasks. I was optimistic about the possibility of love, and this was giving me good vibes right now. I hadn't thought that I missed companionship this much until now.

Marlon was the dude that I had met at the club over two weeks ago. We had been talking on the phone almost every day, getting to know each other. Our conversations were almost always the same, as we discussed over and over our families and our favorite foods, colors, and movies.

This was how our first conversation went.

My phone rang, and my heart fluttered and raced in anticipation.

"Hello," I said when I answered the phone.

"Hey, beautiful," he said.

It felt so good to hear that. It has been a long while since someone besides my friends had loved on me verbally.

"Thanks for the compliment."

"You are worthy of it." His voice made me melt. It was smooth and sensual.

"Okay," I replied. I didn't know what else to say. I didn't want to come across as conceited.

"What were you doing before I called?" he asked.

"Just sipping and listening to some music at home," I answered. I had really been waiting for him to call, but I didn't want to sound desperate.

"You weren't waiting for me to call, were you?"

"Maybe a little bit." I laughed.

"Let me find out that you were dreaming about a brother." He laughed as well.

"I may be guilty of that. One can dream, right?"

"You weren't the only one," he admitted. If he was trying to woo me, then it was working.

"I am glad that we are on the same page," I confessed.

"You are on the front page in my life right now."

"Wow. You are something else," I gushed.

"Nope. I just want to be your everything, if you'll let me."

I was silent. I didn't know what to say to that.

"Hello? Are you still there?" he asked after about thirty seconds of silence.

"Yes, I am still here," I said.

"Did you hear what I just said?" he asked.

"Yes. I didn't know what to say. You caught me off guard."

"I know. I love hard. Life is too short to play around with time," he replied.

"I agree."

"When am going to get to hold you?"

"Hold me?" I asked.

"Yes, I can only imagine how soft you are."

"Oh, my. You are good at this."

"Not really. You just caught my attention, and I have been observing you for a while now. It's like being in your favorite store and not being able to buy anything. I've been wanting to take you home and open you up for a while. Now that I have the opportunity, I will not waste it."

"I hear that. You can continue. Open me up." I laughed.

We continued to talk, and our conversation included going through the basics. You know, likes, loves, and wants. The more we talked, the deeper I fell in love.

After we ended the call, I found myself cleaning up some more because I had invited him over for dinner. I was nervous. I just didn't want to get my hopes up and be let down again.

You just didn't know with people. In my estimation, the honeymoon phase of relationships was very trying. The savviest person could come up short. No one was safe in the dating world.

I didn't go hard in the paint with dinner prepa-rations. My dinner fare consisted of honey-garlic salmon with mashed potatoes and mixed greens. I just wanted him to feel comfortable and intrigued.

I also bought some fresh fruit to munch on while we talked about nothing. You know, small talk. I hoped that I could hold up my end of the conversation better when we were face-to-face than I had over the phone. I was such a shy guy, and I didn't want to be overly anxious.

Around six o'clock there was a knock at the door, which startled me. I walked over to one of my full-length mirrors to make sure that I was still put together. I had on some tight pants and a loose-fitting shirt that had buttons at the top. I had a few open so that he could see the curly hair on my chest.

I opened the door, and his smile sent chills down my spine. He was a thick boy, and I loved it. We were roughly the same height.

"Hey, sir," I greeted him as I stepped back and let him come in the apartment.

"It smells good in here," he said with a smile. "Let me find out that you can cook."

"Well, I do what I do," I said as I walked past him and led him to my living room area. I had the fruit on a small platter on the coffee table, with toothpicks for easy consumption.

"You can have a seat," I said as I motioned for him to sit down on the sofa. I sat down next to him once he was comfortable, leaving some intentional space between us. I didn't want to be all over him. I wanted him to feel comfortable. I also didn't want him to think that I was an easy lay.

I was horny, but I could wait for intimacy. I just wanted to bond and see where it went.

"You have a really nice place here. You must do good for yourself," he commented as he gazed around the room.

"I can't complain. I do what I love. Getting people through tough physical crises uplifts me, and it pays well. It's a great two for one."

"I feel you on that. I love the way music can make people feel better. No matter what they are going through. I feel like it is medicine for the soul. It reaches places that traditional medicine cannot reach."

He was saying all the right things. I was loving him right now.

"Wow, that is an awesome insight, and it is very true. I love it." I smiled hard. I was really feeling this guy. I was hoping that it was mutual.

"You want some fruit?" I asked as I picked up the platter filled with small pieces of melon and strawberries.

"Sure," he answered before he picked up a piece and put it in his mouth. A little juice escaped his lips as he chewed. I wanted to lick it off, but I just offered him a napkin to wipe it off.

"My bad," he said with a smirk. "Look at me acting greedy and messy."

"Marlon, there is no judgment here. I love your freedom to be you. It puts my anxiety at ease. Thanks for being you," I said as I looked him in the eyes.

Out of nowhere he leaned in and kissed me on the lips. I could taste the lingering fruit flavor as he slipped his tongue into my mouth. I matched his intensity. He was now close enough for me to feel his chest on my own.

Seconds later he pulled back and then grabbed another piece of fruit and put it in his mouth.

My chest heaved up and down from the passion and intensity of his kiss. I was stunned.

"I have wanted to do that ever since we sat down. You have some soft lips, bro," he told me.

"Thanks," was all that I could say. I was flattered and horny.

We both fell silent and enjoyed the fruit.

"I hope I wasn't going too fast with the kiss. I couldn't help myself," he admitted, breaking the silence after several minutes had gone by.

"No, you are fine. I thoroughly enjoyed it."

"I don't want you to think that I came over here to get into your pants. I just like what I saw."

"No worries. I like what I felt too. I wasn't worried about sex either. I just want to get to know you, and now I know that you can kiss. That is a good start," I assured him.

He nodded.

"Are you ready for dinner?" I asked.

"Absolutely. It smells good. I am ready."

We moved to the dining area of my apartment, where I had the table set for two. I grabbed the food out of the oven, where it was being kept warm. We sat, ate, and talked some more. We kissed a few more times, and those kisses were just as passionate as the first.

For a while, we just sat still and looked at each other. I didn't know what to say; I just wanted to enjoy the moment.

"Look at you," he said as he looked at me.

"What's wrong with me?" I asked.

"I can't find anything. You are perfect." He put the back of his hand on my cheek and smoothed it across my face. I closed my eyes and enjoyed the moment.

I opened my eyes to him leaning in and kissing me again. I almost instinctively leaned back in the chair so that he could climb on my lap, but I didn't want to rush anything. I didn't want to ruin it by going too fast. Even though I really wanted to go for it.

Nothing other than kisses happened during the rest of our night together. But it was a close call a few times. I was glad that we waited. I really wanted to take it slow and get to know him, and he felt the same way. I was hopeful.

Around ten o'clock I walked him to the door while holding hands with him. I felt like a kid with a crush.

"When am I going to see you again?" he asked as he leaned up against the open door.

The urge to pull him back into the house and go to my knees was strong, but I had some fight in me. I would just have to do it myself tonight.

"I'll give you a call and let you know," I said and then winked at him.

"Oh, I see. You're going to make me wait." He laughed.

"Well, absence does make the heart grow fonder," I said and then smiled.

"I hear that," he said, then returned my smile. He leaned in and kissed me one more time and then walked away.

I closed the door and leaned against the wall and prayed that this was the one.

Chapter 15

Marcus

I was ashamed of myself. I should be. What kind of therapist snuck off with one of his patients' lovers?

That therapist was me.

But shame didn't stop me from going to Walmart to get some Magnum condoms and lubricant. I was too far gone to stop now. Shame didn't stop me from going over to the Hilton Hotel to get my freak on with a stranger. I was no better than a ho prostituting herself.

I checked into a room and then texted the info to Ronald. My anticipation was high. Even though this was a one-night stand type of deal. If he was good with the tools he had, I wouldn't mind throwing a few more nights his way. I would see.

I didn't know how to present myself, so I just stripped down to my boxers and a T-shirt.

Before long there was a knock on the door. I looked through the peephole and then let him in. He came in with the confidence that I had heard about and witnessed at the restaurant the other day. He didn't waste any time getting undressed and letting it all hang out.

His naked body was impressive. He had plenty of muscles on his slender frame. I admired his physique a bit before I walked up to him and rubbed my hand across his chest.

"You like that, don't you?" His voice was husky, and it fueled my lust-filled thoughts.

I just nodded my head and moved down toward his manhood, which had some girth to it.

"Not so fast. Let me hop in the shower quick," he said and walked off. "Can you wash my back?" he asked, looking back, with a flirty smile on his face.

I stripped out of the rest of my clothes and followed right behind him.

It didn't take long before we were lathering each other down with soap, exploring each other's body with intensity. I wanted to feel every crack and crevice on his body. I was searching his body like someone looking for lost money.

"You feel good and soft," he said as he palmed my behind and pulled me close to him. His aggressiveness was a complete turn-on. I loved being in charge, but I loved to be handled sexually.

The water and soap made things slippery and sensual.

"Show me you want it," he whispered in my ear as my hand worked on his already hard manhood.

I pulled him out of the shower by his manhood. I grabbed a towel and methodically dried every inch of his body. He stood there as I paid extra attention to his manhood.

"I think he likes you," he said, and he made it jump and slap his thigh.

"The feeling is mutual."

Ronald grabbed the towel and toweled me down with the same care that I had shown him. I enjoyed every moment of it.

"Let's go make this happen," he said as he walked into the bedroom.

I followed behind him, fully anticipating the passion to come, but my high was interrupted by the ringing of a phone that was not mine.

"Don't pay it no mind. Let it ring," he said as he pulled his cell out of his pants pocket.

My conscience knew who it was or at least who I suspected it to be.

"I sexed her down before I left so that I could come and get a real treat," he confessed and then looked at me. "Let me put this on silent so that we can get it in."

When you know better you are supposed to do better, I thought. I knew better, but I didn't care.

"Now let's get this party started," he said after stuffing his cell back in his pants pocket.

I was already sitting on the bed when he slowly pushed my back toward the mattress. He began fondling me, and soon our limbs became intertwined.

Again, we were interrupted by the ringing of a phone. It was mine this time. He let out a frustrated breath that matched my thoughts.

We unwound ourselves so that I could get to the phone. After turning it off, I put it on the nightstand beside the bed. I didn't have to look at it to know who had called.

I ignored it. I ignored her. I ignored my conscience. I wanted what I wanted.

And I got it.

His performance was everything that I needed and more. He knew how to use everything that God had given him, and I was even more grateful to God for that.

Chapter 16

Evan

I was having a fantastic day. I had already seen a few clients, and most of them were doing what they were supposed to be doing. They didn't make my job of conditioning them any harder than it naturally was. The human body was like a puzzle, and both the mind and the body had to be in line to function optimally.

The lady that I had just finished working with was in her sixties. She was the one who always made it easy for me. Some of my clients half her age struggled to keep it together and maintain a healthy balance outside the gym.

I had rented out a small room in a large gym to provide my services. It was a great gym with plenty of potential clients. I must admit that my good looks had got me a lot of my clients. That and word of mouth. Even though I was messy at times, things never got out of hand, and most people wanted only parts of you, anyway, and not the whole package.

Time flew, and before I knew it, I was cleaning up the room so that I could get ready for my last appointment. I was so ready to go to the club tonight to drink off my stress.

As I was putting away some equipment, Allen popped his head in the door. "Hey, sir."

I couldn't say that I was surprised to see him. He had just had a session yesterday and was scheduled again for later in the week.

"Everything okay?" I asked. I was curious as to why he was here, because we had never discussed additional sessions beyond the two a week he had scheduled. I wasn't opposed to more than two each week, but I usually limit the sessions to that so that my clients could give their bodies time to heal.

"Yes. I just came by to see you." He had a bright smile on his face.

He walked into the room and began to do stretches and other things that I had taught him to do. I looked on as he began to go through the routine that I had coached him on. He was doing all the stretches and techniques that I had taught him. I was impressed but still puzzled.

"You like what you see?" he said as he positioned his legs in an upside-down V and then bent his torso so that it was in between his legs.

"I'm impressed," I said with a grin.

He stood upright and then walked toward me.

"I guess I have to give you more challenging exercises," I told him.

"I know one exercise that I want to practice," he said when he reached me. He grabbed my manhood.

"Stop," I cautioned him. "This is not the place for that. This is my business."

"You didn't say that when we exchanged sexual favors." He looked at me and then seductively put his finger in his mouth and pulled it out.

"That was a mistake. We shouldn't have done that."

"It didn't feel like a mistake. You wanted it. You wanted me."

"Allen, I have a client who is about to come. Can we discuss this later? I will call you," I said as I walked toward the door.

"You promise?" he said as he walked up to me in the doorway.

"Yes."

"Cool." He quickly kissed me on the lips, leaving me stunned in the doorway. I prayed that no one had seen this.

This guy was really pushing for a relationship, but I really didn't want to pursue one right now. I didn't want to be tied down to any one person. I was committed to myself. That was all I wanted.

Later that night . . .

I needed as much liquor as I could drink tonight after what had happened earlier. And I couldn't even share it with my boys, because they had warned me that this could be a consequence of pooping where you ate.

I danced in my chair to a Cher song that was pumping through the speakers.

"How was your day?" Justin asked me.

"It was interesting, to say the least." A faint chuckle escaped my lips. I had to do a lot of pretending tonight. I felt like a fool.

"Like how?" He looked at me intently. Justin could be needy at times. But I was quick on my feet.

"One of my clients came in drunk and still wanted me to service her." I shook my head and blew out a fake frustrated breath.

"Wow." He looked at me with a shocked expression on his face.

"Yeah, she was in a dual class with two other chicks, but I had to pay more attention to her than the others. Surprisingly, she was doing better than the other two." I laughed.

"Really?" Justin was drunk already. I didn't even think he was paying attention. One giveaway was that he had a goofy smile on his face. One that only alcohol could give you, or some good love.

"Yep. But I made it through the day, and here I am."

Keith and Marcus were on the dance floor, dancing away their stress. They looked like they were having the time of their lives.

I continued to drink and drown my regret. I didn't have the foggiest idea how to handle this situation. I decided that I was going to keep this to myself until I got this under control.

Chapter 17

Keith

"Keith," Jennifer said as she came into my office. She plopped down in the chair in front of my desk. She had an intent look on her face.

"How can I help you?" I gazed back at her with the same look on my face.

"Kingston," she said, singing his name. "Shaba." She jokingly threw in a Jamaican accent, which made me laugh.

"Jennifer, you are crazy."

"No, just horny." She laughed.

"I agree."

"That man is the man of my dreams. I'm ready to have all his kids," she gushed.

"Oh, really?"

"Yes, honey. He wined and dined me. It was so good, I was getting ready to get down on one knee and propose to him."

"Girl, stop." I waved a hand at her. "It was that good?" I asked.

"Keith, that man was giving all the signs that he wanted more than just work ethic and productivity. He was giving me a fever. It was ninety degrees every time he smiled. I had to go to the bathroom and wring out my panties, he made me so wet." She fell over laughing.

"Jennifer, leave that man alone. He doesn't want you. He's a businessman who was conducting business. Your imagination is in overdrive."

I didn't know if I said this for her benefit or my own.

"I know that you are not being a hater, right?" She glared at me.

"No. I just think that you should back up a bit. I don't want you to embarrass yourself if this is not a mutual attraction," I said, making my opinion clear.

"I appreciate the concern, but I'm a grown woman. This is not my first rodeo when dealing with a man of his caliber," she stated with confidence.

"I didn't mean to offend you," I said, apologizing.

"Keith, I know that it came from a good place. At least I hope so." And then she laughed. I did as well.

"Jen, I thought you were about swing at me for a second there," I joked.

"Boo, you never know. I will fight over a good piece of a man now. You already know."

"I hear you, and I don't want no smoke." I sat back in my chair.

"Let me get back to work," Jennifer said, and then she exited my office as quickly as she'd come in.

I sat back in my chair and thought about Kingston and the way he treated me. It was a great feeling to be wanted. I really wasn't looking for someone or a relationship. It was amazing how we found stuff that we were not looking for.

I had to agree with Jennifer. He was a fine specimen. But I would be cautious around him, as I had told her to be. It would be crazy for me not to take my own advice.

Life was about taking chances. However, I wasn't ready to take any chances. I didn't think now was the time.

Chapter 18

Justin

I felt like a kid in a candy store. All that I could think about was Marlon. Some moments during the day, I just lost focus and daydreamed. I was floating on cloud nine. I wanted to punch myself to see if it was all a dream.

I was already attentive to my patients, and this week they had been getting extra-special treatment. A budding relationship would do that for you. I couldn't believe my feelings right now. My expectations were off the hook. I was already planning my life around him and me.

We had been texting back and forth. Just getting to know your stuff. Dreams and aspirations. Fears and failures. I was putting it all on the table.

I was at home now, getting ready to go see him at one of his club events. My boys would be there, but they wouldn't know that I was involved with the DJ. I wanted to keep things under wraps until

I was sure things were on a sure footing. I didn't want to be out there embarrassing myself.

For so long, I had prided myself on being an optimistic person, but it had been proven to me that I wasn't that person. I was a pessimistic person to the core. It seemed like my thoughts sabotaged everything in my life before it got good.

I had way too much time to think. My imagination was on high alert most of the time. I probably should have been an author or something, because I could create a scene in my head and determine the way that I wanted it to go. It felt like every phone call that I got would bring news of a death or other really bad news. I didn't want to answer the phone, because I wasn't sure if I could handle the news the person on the other end of the line might deliver.

So, Marlon was a dream come true. He seemed so sweet and genuinely interested in me and my life. No, I didn't see him coming. I was surprised he even had any interest in me. After all, I considered myself the boring one in my group of friends. All I did was work, eat, and go home. The club life was one of the only outlets I had with my friends. With all of us having our own businesses and being so successful, we needed the escape.

Thanks to Marlon, there was such a seesaw of emotions going on in my head. I didn't want to ruin this budding relationship. I wanted to make this work. It felt like this was my last chance at a real love life. Sometimes I told myself that I was going to make this work and leave caution to the wind, as they said. But I wasn't as confident as I would have liked.

Yes, I thought I was handsome, but was I interesting enough to keep a man? I didn't want to be in a relationship where all I had to offer was sex. I loved sex. Who didn't? I just didn't want it to be the basis for a relationship. I wanted to be able to mesh with Marlon on all levels. Mentally, physically, and spiritually.

Was that too much for me to ask? Would God honor this request? I was hoping that He would. I was a good guy, and so why wouldn't God look out for me? I treated His people like I wanted to be treated.

A few times this week I had found myself pleading with God to let this work out. To let this be the one for me. I thought I deserved this love. I knew I deserved this love.

Later that night . . .

My boys and I were sitting at a table, but my focus was on Marlon the whole time. He was up in the booth that they had for the DJ who was doing his thing. The music he was playing had hyped the crowd up, and we were enjoying it as well.

"Whoever is playing the music tonight is doing his thing," I said. Complimenting my man on the low was exhilarating.

"Yeah, he is doing it up," Keith said as he got out of his seat and headed toward the dance floor.

Evan and Marcus followed Keith over to the dance floor, and I watched from my seat as my boys danced out of their minds to a Cardi B hit.

I felt like I was on top of the world. It seemed like all was right in my world.

Then I heard over the speaker, "This goes out to a special person in the crowd tonight. You the one, boo." "Everything to Me," by Monica, came on.

That was all I needed to make my night go right. I was smiling extra hard now. I swayed to Monica's sultry voice as she sang her heart out. She was one of my favorite female singers.

"I got one more for you, boo," he said as he put on another one of my favorites.

"Chanté's Got a Man," by Chanté, just sent me even further into my feelings. I felt like a star whose light could never be dimmed. I sang along to the song, as did many other people in the room. They didn't know that it was for me only. I just enjoyed the private spotlight.

When the song was over, my boys came back to the table.

"Aren't those two of your favorite songs?' Evan asked as he sat down at the table.

I just nodded my head and swayed to the music that was still playing in my head.

"You would have thought that he was talking about you or something," Evan mused.

"Nah, it's just a coincidence. Nobody checking for me like that." I faked a frown.

"Boy, cut that out. I see guys checking you out all the time," Evan asserted. "You are just too slow to catch on. You're a hot boy. Not as hot as me, but you are pulling them too. Just open your eyes."

"I will start. I promise." I nodded my head in agreement.

Chapter 19

Marcus

"I think Ronald is cheating on me," my patient said to me as soon she and I sat down. She had a frustrated look on her face.

"Melissa, what makes you think that?" I asked. I couldn't wait to see what her answer would be. I didn't think that she was a dumb woman, just a desperate one.

"All this overattentive behavior. And then, the other day, he sexed me so good that I passed out and woke up to him being gone. I called his phone a few times, and he never answered."

"Well, isn't that his pattern?" I reminded her. Pangs of guilt fluttered in my stomach, but I ignored them. I was not her problem. Ronald was her problem. He was just a sexual fix for me. A means to release my sexual frustration without a commitment. She was committed to his shenanigans, not me.

"Yes, but why would he be all over me one minute and then disappear the next?"

"He's unstable. What do you expect?" I looked at her intently.

She didn't say anything as a few tears fell down her face. This tugged at my ethics. The ones that I had been ignoring.

Finally, she spoke. "Why won't he just be a good man? I mean, I am a good woman. I give him everything that he needs and wants."

"Okay." I nodded my head to communicate that I wasn't agreeing with her, but I was actively listening. "How do you know that everything you give is all that he needs?" I proposed. I knew that it wasn't, but did she?

"I'm a woman. I'm supplying all his needs. I keep him coming back." She sounded confident. She believed it. Or at least she made me believe that she believed it.

"I admire your confidence." I wasn't cosigning anything she had said, because what she had said was foolish. I just let her do her. Being a therapist didn't mean I had answers for her. Nor did I have to agree with her choices. I was here to listen and give some insight. That was it. That was all.

"Do you have this problem with men?" She looked at me like she expected that I was really going to go into my personal business in front of her.

"Melissa, we both lead very different lives, and it wouldn't be smart of me to compare notes. I must keep this professional, or you will not benefit from my services," I reminded her.

"Doc, you are on the money. That's why I trust you with my secrets. I know that you aren't going to use them or me. I appreciate that."

"That is my job, and I love my job." It sounded good coming out of my mouth.

"I'm so glad that you love your job, because I need you every step of the way. Even with some of my crazy decisions, you don't judge me. That is very important to me."

"We all have faults, so I can't judge you. We need each other."

"My time is up," she said as she looked at her watch. "Until next time."

"Until next time," I repeated.

I watched as she exited my office. Then I sat back in my chair and closed my eyes.

The guilt still ate at my soul. But I pushed it aside as I was in dangerous waters, and I was enjoying the turbulence.

I made a reservation for a sex fest with Ronald tomorrow. After the first two times in one night, my body was craving what he offered. Just thinking about it sent me into sexual overdrive.

Chapter 20

Evan

I tapped my fingers on the table that I was sitting at as I waited for my guest to arrive. This wasn't a date. At least I hoped that it wasn't a date.

I had purposely picked a restaurant that was not my norm but was busy. I didn't know what was going to happen. I had to tell Allen that we had a casual thing between us. That I wasn't looking for a relationship. I wasn't completely reckless when I sleep with men. But with Allen, I had slipped up and hadn't given him the farewell speech that I gave people when we finished.

I felt a little sorry for Allen, because he reminded me of me in some areas of his life. It wasn't really pitying sex. He was cute and attractive, but he was a little young for me, and he didn't seem stable. I had my own issues with being entangled in someone else's problems.

I purposely sat facing the front door so that I could watch him as he came into the restaurant. As soon as he entered, he scanned the room and quickly spotted me. His face lit up, and then he walked toward me. A slight smile covered my face, to be polite to him. I didn't want to frown or show the agitation that I was feeling.

I had to play this right so that this didn't go left. He didn't look like the crazy type. But then again, crazy didn't have a look.

"Hey, Evan," he said as he pulled out a chair and sat down.

"How are you, Allen?" I didn't really care. The question was a formality. I wanted this to be over with as quickly as possible.

"I'm glad to see you. Thanks for the invite."

"No problem," I lied. Then I got right down to business. "I need to talk to you about the scene you caused the other day." I looked him dead in the eyes as I spoke to him. No smile or smirk. I needed to let him know that I was serious.

"I loved every moment of it. Didn't you?" He looked like he was in heaven as he gazed at me. It softened my stance a bit.

"I don't conduct myself that way at work. I could lose clients that way. I was lucky that no one was around or paying attention."

"Oh, my bad. I don't want to jeopardize your income or clients. I just want to show you how much

I like you. You accepted me, and I am grateful for that." His voice shook as he spoke. He was getting emotional, and I couldn't let him down now.

"Thanks for understanding. I just wanted you to know that I must keep it professional at work. I don't want anyone to get the misconception that I sleep with clients. It could get messy for me. I don't need that," I explained.

"I will not put you in that position again," he assured me. "You don't do that someone you love."

"Love?" I asked. I was blown away by the use of the word. We humans threw that word around quite a bit. Mostly, we lied when we said it.

"Yes, love. You made me feel again. I didn't want to love again, but you broke through my wall, and now I can love again."

He was serious, and I was scared. He had developed feelings for me extremely fast.

"I don't know what to say," I said honestly.

"You don't have to say a thing," he assured me. "I know that this is fast. But I can't deny my feelings for you. And I know that you feel something for me as well. Don't worry. You don't have to make any confessions. I will prove my love to you, and that will draw you closer to me. Love is here for you. I am here for you. So, let's just enjoy a meal together and let love lead the way."

"Okay," was all that I could get out. I was stunned. Confused and stunned.

Chapter 21

Keith

I was sitting in my office, working on some last-minute emails, when there was a knock on my door.

"Come in," I called out.

"Keith, am I bothering you?" Kingston asked as he came in. His cologne entered the room before he did. It was like Folger's coffee. It woke up everything in me.

"Not at all." I motioned for him to have a seat.

He sat down and then crossed his legs.

He dressed like the professional that he presented himself to be. His smooth-looking dark skin and chiseled square chin gave off very confident vibes. He was a man who was sure of himself but did not overdo it.

He was one of God's masterpieces. His suit had been made for him and highlighted his firm arms and thighs. He looked like he was staying long at the gym.

"How are you doing today?" he asked. Holding his gaze as we sat face-to-face was hard for me. I had to keep it professional with him. But my lust for him was not making it easy.

"I am doing well."

"I came in here to have a one-on-one with you."

My mind instantly went to a vision of him and me having sex in my office with my door closed. I could feel the heat of his breath as he ravaged my body with kisses. His massive arms pinned me to the desk as he had his way with me.

"Oh, okay." I sat up in my chair. I wanted to be alert and attentive to his every word.

"I'm so glad that you have the ambition and the drive that is needed to take you higher in the company. You are who I have been looking for. I have some friends in high places, and I can't wait for them to meet you."

"Meet me?" I questioned.

"Yes. Don't be nervous. I am going to take very good care of you."

He stood up from the chair. "I will keep you posted on the details. Have a good evening and rest up." He smiled.

He exited my office; I got up and closed my door. I sat back down and looked out my office window. I didn't know what to think. I was nervous. I didn't know what to expect.

I was glad I was getting my wish. I really wanted to have a positive impact on this company and move up in the world. My future looked much brighter now that Kingston had stepped into this place.

Finally, it was happening.

Finally.

I hit the club up by myself that night. I was excited to be moving forward in my life. Having a man right now would be great, but I would worry about that at another time.

I was in a corner booth, with a drink in my hand, swaying to the soft R & B music that came out of the speakers. A minute later, "On & On," by Erykah Badu, came on, causing me to sway a bit harder.

It was good to just be in the club and not have to deal with another situation or problem. I missed my boys, but I knew that I would catch up with them another day.

I opened Instagram on my phone and made a live video of me jamming in a club. I was high on alcohol and life. I was loving it. A few people commented about the music and encouraged me to have a good time.

I was truly enjoying myself. I got up out of my seat and made my way to the dance floor, where I danced and continued to share my experience with my friends online.

"Hey . . . hey . . . hey . . . hey," I chanted when a Biggie classic came on. I was hype, as they said.

After dancing to a few more songs, I made my way over to the bar to refill my drink and then returned to my booth. There were some cuties in the house tonight, and as I sat and enjoyed my drink, I made sure I enjoyed all the eye candy in the room.

I loved coming to the club. Whether to celebrate or to decompress, this was the place to be. Some people went to church or to restaurants. The club was where my boys and I let loose and bonded. A good drink could be found here. A good laugh could be found here. A good time could be found here. And even a good cry could be found here.

Chapter 22

Justin

Marlon was sitting across the table from me with his fine self. I almost couldn't contain myself. I was over the moon in love. It was the kind of love that you knew was real. I felt it as soon as I woke up in the morning, and it laid me down to sleep at night.

"I'm so glad that I finally approached you," he revealed.

I was so nervous. "Really?" I gushed.

"Yes, you seemed so out of my league," he confessed.

"No one has ever said that to me before." I was smiling, and I felt like singing a love song right now. I couldn't sing, so that was out of the question.

"Justin, you are it. All that I need." He reached out and grabbed my hand with both of his. He squeezed with such intensity. I felt the love that he was confessing.

"I'm speechless. I receive everything that you are saying. I needed to hear this. I have been waiting for this all my life. There have been many people who said they wanted me, but only to get a quick hit, and then they disappeared." I felt more emotions well up in me. A tear slid down my face. I lowered my head and let a few more tears fall. They were tears of release. All the pain, fear, and regret were escaping, and I was happy about it.

"I don't know about what you have been through, but I am here to erase it all away." He pulled my hand toward him and then kissed it.

I looked around the restaurant and at all the people who surrounded us, and I felt like I was the luckiest one in the room. There were other couples sitting at tables, and they looked like they were in love. I was so glad to now be among them.

I had a man. I had a man who cared for me.

He hadn't asked for sex or even forced his way on me. He was a perfect gentleman.

"I can't believe that you are finally here." I smiled as I looked him in the eyes. "Who knew that going to a club would land me a man like you? I can't believe it."

"Believe it. I'm the real deal. I love hard. I love long. It's me and you against the world."

"Me and you," I repeated.

"Against the world," he added, following up.

We ordered our food and talked for what seemed like hours. I wanted to pinch myself.

We left the restaurant in separate cars that night, and I was so bubbly on the ride home.

It was my turn for love. My turn for life. No one could burst my bubble. I would keep this from Evan, Keith, and Marcus until I felt like telling them.

Chapter 23

Marcus

In another hotel room.

More mind-blowing sex.

More unanswered phone calls.

It seemed like Melissa knew when we were about to get it in, since at that moment, she would call. I was too determined to get what I wanted. She was determined to keep the one who didn't want her.

She would call him, and then she would call me.

I so wanted to tell her to chill out and leave us alone. She didn't know that I didn't want him for good. He was a serviceman.

A man with a service.

Supply and demand.

He knew his role, and I knew mine.

Ronald and I were both naked in the bed. It was silent in the room. We both were spent.

"I need a favor," Ronald said, breaking the silence.

"What kind of favor?" I asked.

"I need some money."

"Money? I don't exchange sex for money," I said as I sat up on the side of the bed.

"I just need it to get something for Melissa for her birthday. I didn't want to ask her for money to buy a gift for her. That's not a good look."

This guy really was something. He wanted me to give him money for a girl whom he was cheating on. I felt even more foolish to even be in this situation. All these people that I counseled daily, and I was out here living just as recklessly.

"That's not something that I can do," I said as I turned around and looked at him with a straight face.

"Even after I just sexed you down with this good wood?" He waved his now-limp manhood at me.

"Unfortunately, that is the case. We exchanged sexual favors. I believe that is a fair trade."

He stood up and began to get dressed. He was quiet, so I guessed he didn't want to press the issue.

"I didn't want to do this, but you leave me no choice," he said as he walked up to me while I was still sitting on the bed.

He pulled his wallet out of his back pocket and then took a card out of it. He handed it to me. It was one of my business cards. "I know that you are Melissa's therapist," he said and smiled.

I frowned.

"You're a therapist. I'm an opportunist." He laughed.

I didn't like where this was going.

"Is this blackmail?" I muttered, glaring at him.

"That sounds so harsh. Let's call it what you did. A fair exchange. I'm pretty sure that it's a violation to sleep with a client's boyfriend. Don't worry. I looked it up, and it is."

I just nodded my head in disappointment.

"I'm pretty sure you want to keep your license and business. Because I do have text messages from you that would confirm it all. And Melissa would not be too pleased to find out this information."

"True," was all that I could say. He was right again.

"Don't worry. Our Melissa won't find out as long as we stay on the same page."

"No problem," I muttered.

"I'm going to have to go shopping for Melissa's gift. Can you help me out now?"

"How much do you think it will cost?" I asked.

"Check your wallet and let's see." He laughed again.

I picked my pants up off the floor to retrieve my wallet. I opened it to see what cash I had inside. His impatience caused him to snatch the wallet from my hand. He took all the cash that was in it.

He counted it in front of me like he was a pimp. I felt like a prostitute.

"This is all that you have?" he asked.

"I don't carry a lot of cash," I replied. I couldn't even look him in the eye.

"A hundred dollars will have to do for the moment." He gave another laugh.

There was silence on my end.

"I'll hit you up for more when I need it. You have Apple Pay or Zelle?"

"Yes," I answered.

"Cool. I'll be in touch."

He walked out of the hotel room with the bop of a hustler.

I had just got hustled.

I fell back on the bed and covered my face with my hands. Book smarts and street smarts were two different things. I had been robbed without a gun. As the saying went, "It's all fun until the rabbit has the gun."

I finally got up out of the bed and slowly dressed myself. After I put on my shirt, I sat on the side of the bed, shaking my head from side to side. I should have just walked out of the hotel without any clothes on, because that was how low I felt. I didn't think that I would have cared about the looks I got. Embarrassed did not describe how I felt. I was mortified. Here I was with all this wisdom, and I couldn't control my hormones. I was acting like a horny teenager and had got caught up in some mess. I didn't even think I could get out of this mess without losing everything.

As the saying went, I was up a creek without a paddle.

Chapter 24

Evan

I sat on the side of the bed, drunk from imbibing heavily at the club tonight. I hadn't drunk too much for fun this time. I'd drunk too much because I was still confused about Allen.

I felt like I was getting punked or something. This felt like a relationship. A relationship that I was not looking for. I mean, the boy was cute and all, but I didn't want to commit to anyone. I wanted to be a free bird. I liked coming and going as I pleased. I was a grown man, and I wasn't about to be forced into anything I did not want to be in. I didn't care how nice he was to me.

There was a knock at my door. It was after two o'clock in the morning. I was not in the mood for any foolishness. I walked to the door, looked through the peephole, and saw that Allen was standing on the other side. He had bags of food in his hands.

I stood back and blew out a frustrated breath. Then I hesitantly opened the door.

"Hey, love." He gave me a big smile as he walked past me into my apartment. *My* apartment.

I quickly caught up to him and stopped him by pulling at the back of his shirt. "What's going on?" I asked as I looked at the bags in his hands.

"A midnight snack," he said as he turned back toward me. He held the bags up so that I could see them better. I got a good look at the bags, which said IHOP on them.

My stomach involuntarily growled. I was hungry. I was confused all over again. How did he know that I would be hungry? Was he following me? My boys and I frequented many clubs, and I had never told him where I would be tonight.

"I knew that you were at the club late, and figured that you would be hungry, so I stopped and picked up something for you to eat. This food will help with the hangover."

I stood there in the middle of my apartment floor, speechless. I couldn't believe the audacity of him thinking he knew what I liked. I wanted to be mad at him and put him out, but I was drunk *and* hungry. Food was a weakness for me. I made a mental note to discuss my concerns with him when I sobered up.

"Don't worry. Just go sit at the dining room table, and I will plate this for you. Don't forget to wash your hands." He walked toward my kitchen before I could say anything in response.

I did as I was told, because I really couldn't argue with him. I was hungry, and he was feeding me. I admitted to myself that I didn't like this aggressiveness, but I rode with it to see where this might go. I might like it.

The night didn't finish there, though. This boy was all about service. After he served me my food, he disappeared. A few minutes went by, and I heard running water. He came back into the room and sat down in front of me and watched me finish my food. He had a goofy love face on. I had to admit that it was cute.

"I have a bath running for you when you finish," he told me.

"A bath?" I asked. He was going all in on this "Serve me" piece.

"Yes. You probably danced hard tonight."

"Yes, I did do that." I smiled at the memory of me getting it in on the dance floor. I had had a good time tonight.

"I poured some of the liquid Epsom salt from the soap basket next to your tub in the water."

"Thanks." I smiled. I loved taking baths that had Epsom and bubbles. That stuff really worked for minor aches and pains.

Before he spoke again, he waited until I looked like I was finished eating. "I'll clean this up while you go and bathe."

I got up from the table and then walked down the hall that led to my bathroom. I stopped and looked back at Allen while he cleaned up the table. I shook my head at how I was letting this guy treat me like a pushover. I continued toward the bathroom.

My mouth dropped as I walked into the bathroom. He had lit a few candles, and bubbles were floating on top of the bathwater. He had also put my bath pillow in the tub so that I could relax and all. I was impressed. Impressed and nervous. It felt like I had no control. This was new to me. I was always in control.

I had been in the tub for about twenty minutes and most of the bubbles had disappeared when, like magic, Allen appeared with a fresh towel and a bottle of oil.

"Here is a towel and some oil for you," he said.

"Thanks." I looked at him and shook my head.

"What's wrong?" he asked. It looked like he was concerned.

"Why are you doing all of this?" I finally asked. It was too much.

"Because you looked out for me, and I wanted to do the same for you. This is going to be a give-and-take relationship. This is love looking out for you." He walked up to me, bent down, and kissed me on the lips. He had some soft lips. Very soft lips.

Not long after he left the bathroom, I climbed out of the tub, toweled off, oiled my body up, and headed toward the bedroom. The food and bath were good. The combination of them both made me feel like a newborn baby ready for bed.

I walked into my bedroom to newly changed linens on my bed. Allen was standing at the foot of the bed.

"I found these in your linen closet and thought you should have a freshly made bed after you bathed," he announced.

"Thanks," I said as I sat down on the bed.

"I'm going to go home now. I'll see you soon." He walked toward the bedroom door.

"Wait," I said.

"What's wrong?" He walked back toward me.

"What's going on here? Why are you doing all of this?" I asked.

"I am doing this for us. For you." He smiled. His eyes said that he was sincere.

"What do you mean when you say *us*?" I asked.

"Well, I know that you are not looking for a commitment, but I am going to be committed for both of us. I am going to win you over."

I didn't know what else to say. He was trying to do just that. And succeeding. He was winning me over, but I wasn't going to tell him that out loud.

"Okay," was all that I could say.

I walked him to the front door and then made my way back to my bedroom.

I kicked myself for not getting some sex before he left. That was all I needed to really end my night. I wasn't sure where this was going, but I liked the beginning of it. I would just wait and see.

Chapter 25

Keith

"Hey, Mom. Hey, Dad." I said, greeting my adoptive parents as they opened the front door for me.

I was happy to see them. I didn't visit them as often as I should, but these trips meant the world to me when I got the chance.

Cheryl and Morgan Adams took me in when I was about fourteen years old. It was a surprise adoption, because most kids didn't get adopted at that age and older. Couples generally wanted to adopt younger kids. I guessed it made the transition easier.

I didn't want to leave my boys, because we got on so well together. But that didn't stop me from taking the chance at a new life. I made a pact to stay bonded with them, and this was easy since the Adamses didn't live far from where I was enrolled in school.

It didn't hurt that we already had the same last name. It was a match made in heaven. The Adamses were very accepting of my sexuality, but they gave me boundaries and rules that shaped me to this day. They even paid for my college tuition and a new car.

They were not rich, but they worked hard as professional chefs. They owned two restaurants, which I worked in to earn some of my way through college. The Adamses paid most of my college tuition, and they even bought me a car. They were committed to my education and did all they could to prepare me for the future.

"Hey, son." My mother stepped outside and kissed me on the cheek.

"To what do we owe this honor?" My father followed my mother, then grabbed me around the shoulders and ushered me into the house.

"A son can't come and see his parents?" I beamed at them.

"Okay, what do you want?" My mother grabbed my hand and kissed it. I felt the love. It had never wavered.

"You know I come here hungry." I laughed as I made my way to the kitchen. There was always a delicious food dish waiting for guests.

I smiled as soon as I opened the refrigerator door and saw all the good food waiting for me. "Yum, lasagna," I cooed. It was one of my favorite dishes, and my mother always made it to perfection.

"I think she knew you were coming," my father said from behind me as I put the dish of lasagna on the counter.

"I heard that," my mother said as she came in the kitchen.

My father and I laughed as we both reached for plates to dish our lasagna onto. We heated up the food and then sat down at the spacious kitchen table to talk.

There was no place like home.

I instantly turned into the young teenager that I was when I first arrived at this house. My first days here were a bit rocky, because I didn't want to do anything that might give them a reason to take me back to the group home. But that never happened.

The kitchen was the most inviting room in the house. This was where they instilled in me many of the values I adhered to today. In this kitchen they told me stories of their upbringing and never shied away from the tough lessons.

There wasn't a day in this household that I didn't feel welcome, and the Adamses opened our door to my friends as well.

"So how is my baby doing in the big ole world?" My mother laid her head on top of mine as she stood behind.

"I think I am doing pretty well," I said, and then I scooped some food into my mouth. It seemed like the ingredients melted in my mouth. I was so glad to be back home. It was like taking a break from the world. I could really block out all the business of the world when I came home.

"I'm sure you are, son." My father looked at me, pride in his eyes. It felt good to have parents who were proud of me. No matter what age I was, my parents were always a source of inspiration.

I looked down at my plate, and it was empty.

"You want some more?" my mother asked. Before I could answer, she grabbed my plate and began filling it again.

She knew what I liked, and she didn't deviate from it most of the time. While I was a teenager, she was very attentive and loving toward me, something a fearful boy needed. My father showed his love by imposing rigid rules to keep me on track and acting stern when it was called for.

Before long, my plate was empty again. "I'm going to go upstairs and take a nap," I said as I pushed away from the table.

"Sure, baby. Everything is the way you left it in your room," my mother said as she rubbed my back.

I left the table, climbed the stairs, and made my way to the room that I had called home during high school and college. I took off my shoes and flopped on the bed, as I had as a teenager.

It felt so good to be home.

A few hours later I woke up in the bed that had cultivated some of my dreams.

My mother peeked her head through the cracked door. "Hey, sleepyhead. Did you sleep well?"

I yawned and stretched before I answered. "It was nice." I smiled and sat up. I stretched a bit more, because it was quite restful.

"I checked on you a couple of times and was tempted to wake you. You looked so cute that I left you alone." She smiled at me.

"Great choice," I said and laughed.

She came over to the bed and sat down beside me. "Is everything okay?"

"Yes, it is." I felt like it was on the inside.

"I hope so," she said as she gazed at me. "Your father and I were concerned because you generally don't pop up like this."

"I know. This is one of my safe places. I just need a break from the world. You know?" I looked at her in the eyes.

"That I do." She nodded her head, then stood up and left the room.

It didn't take me long to get up and splash some water on my face. This was time well spent for me. I needed it.

Chapter 26

Justin

It was date night, and Marlon surprised me with a trip down to National Harbor, which was close to Washington DC. This was one of my favorite places to go. When we got there, the crowd was light, probably because the weather was cool.

Marlon and I were taking it slow when it came to our relationship. We both preferred it that way. Getting to know someone was a process. Most people nowadays just wanted to get right to the physical part. I had to admit that I was curious about that part, but I had to wait.

Marlon was a handsome dude. Not overly handsome, but good enough for me. He was taller than me. We both had a dark caramel complexion. He had an extended beard, and my face was clean shaven. I thought we looked good together.

"You like the view?" he asked.

We were on the boardwalk, sitting next to each other on a wooden bench and looking out at the water. It was great to just listen to the sounds of nature and breathe in the fresh air.

"I adore it." I put my head on his shoulder, closed my eyes, and just breathed in his masculine scent. The cologne he had on intoxicated me.

"I adore you," he whispered.

It was music to my ears. My heart fluttered in my chest. I was really falling for him.

"Do you really mean that?" I asked as I lifted my head off his shoulder.

"Of course I mean it. Where am I right now? I'm with you, and you are with me. You have my full attention. The spotlight is on you, babe." He put his hand under my chin, leaned in, and kissed me.

"Did you feel that?" he asked. "That was me and you connecting. I want more of that. Do you want more of that?" He intently looked in my eyes and didn't move, waiting for me to answer.

"Yes, I want all of it." I smiled.

"It's too late. You already got it." He laughed.

"You are too good to be true." I rubbed his face with my hand.

"You ready to eat?" he asked, changing the topic.

"Yes. I am starving."

"Good. Let's go look for some good eats."

I had a taste for pasta, so we ended up eating at a nice Italian restaurant. As we were seated at a table, I inhaled the scent of Italian seasonings, which filled the room. Italian instrumental music played in the background.

"This is a nice place," Marlon commented as he stared at me from across the table.

I blushed. "You make every place seem nice," I replied, flirting with him.

"This is true." He gave a laugh.

"Do you believe in love at first sight?" I asked.

"Yes, I do. Especially when it involves that behind of yours." He smiled.

I blushed again. "I will take that answer." I reached across the table and rubbed his hand. "Have you ever been in love before?" I asked.

"I thought so," he answered.

"What happened?" I asked.

"Well, it is hard to talk about." He lowered his head. I could feel his pain.

"I know that all too well. Heartbreak is such a touchy subject. No one wants to rehash the pain of a breakup. Especially if you really thought that that person was the one you wanted to spend the rest of your life with."

Fresh memories of my past flooded my mind. Getting over a love loss could be traumatic and lengthy.

"Heartbreak isn't for the faint of heart. It will make or break you," he mused. He looked like he was deep in thought.

"Don't worry. We can get over those together. We can heal together," I assured him.

We ate dinner and talked more about life and other things. It was just nice to have someone that I could just talk to about anything.

"I have one more surprise for you," Marlon said after we had had dessert. As he spoke, he focused on my face and rubbed my left hand, which was on the table.

Butterflies filled my stomach. Was he getting ready to pop the question? I wondered. But I just knew that this would not be happening now. It had been only a few weeks since we started dating.

Tears welled up in my eyes. I could feel my emotions getting the best of me. The yes was already on the tip of my tongue. He was the one. I was his "the one." This was it.

"I'm ready." I smiled with anticipation.

"I rented us a room for the night, so we can get closer."

"Wow." I faked complete excitement. My heart was a bit crushed. There I went again, rushing things. I had set my expectations too high, and now boom. I was dissatisfied with his news. I could kick myself.

After we left the restaurant, we walked the short distance to the hotel where he had booked a room for us. The elegance of the lobby took away most of my disappointment from earlier. We headed up to the room he had booked, and when we walked through the door, it was clear to me that he had been here before.

"I set this all up just for you. I am going to treat you like the king that you are," Marlon told me.

I was genuinely surprised. I had to admit that the room was nice and comfy. I knew it was not cheap. He had paid good money, and I was going to enjoy it.

"I love it!" I exclaimed as I looked around.

"First, we are going to shower together, and then I am going to give you the massage of your life," he announced.

"Marlon, you are amazing." I walked up to him and put my arms around his neck and leaned in for a kiss. It was a deeply passionate kiss.

"All right now. Get them clothes off so we can clean each other up," he said, and he began to take off his own clothes.

Once we were naked, we stood in the middle of the room, looking at each other's body. I was impressed with my own body, but he was in great shape. I thought even Evan would be very impressed.

I walked up to Marlon and slowly rubbed my hand down his chest toward his flat stomach. He didn't have a six-pack, but his abs were very tight and smooth. Next, I looked down at his manhood. He was a nice size, and he wasn't even aroused.

"You like what you see?" I asked him.

"I absolutely do. You are rocking it, baby. God blessed you." He eased his hand around my body and squeezed my behind. He pulled me in and kissed my neck. He was turning me on, and my manhood responded.

He pulled away and then took me by the arm and pulled me in the direction of the bathroom. He turned on the shower, and we waited a few moments to get the temperature to where we wanted it.

We got in the shower, and we took turns lathering each other up and washing away the suds. We took our time and paid close attention to every crack and crevice in each other's body. We excluded our manhood so that we would not be tempted to go all the way. We had both agreed to wait on sex. After we both exited the shower, we dried each other off.

"Are you ready for your massage?" Marlon asked.

"Oh, yes, baby!" I gushed. I was enjoying this intimacy.

"All right. Go lie on the bed. Face down."

I did as I was instructed. Anticipation filled my mind as I lay down on the bed. I hadn't had a massage before, and I was looking forward to it. I was in heaven.

I felt the bed shift as Marlon crawled onto it. I felt him straddle me, and then I felt a liquid being poured onto my back.

It didn't take long before Marlon began to knead the oil into my back and work his way down my body.

"Mmm," I moaned in pleasure as he worked my behind like a pile of fresh bread dough.

"You like?" he asked.

"I love," I replied.

Next, he worked on my legs and then headed down to my feet. I was a ticklish person. I giggled and squirmed as he worked on my feet.

"Roll over, baby," he requested.

I obeyed. I closed my eyes and let him work on the front of my body just as he had done on the back. He was good at this.

Half an hour later I moaned in pleasure as he finished working me over. I loved this intimacy. It was different, but it was challenging not to go all the way.

After he finished with me, I rubbed him down with the same oil that he had used on me.

Later, we both lay on the bed together, our bodies gleaming. I cradled his body with my own. His warmth lulled me to sleep.

Chapter 27

Marcus

"Good morning, Melissa," I said as she sat down in the chair across from me. This was no different than any other session—except for the fact that her boyfriend was now blackmailing me to keep the secret we had.

"Hey, Doc," she said, bursting with excitement. I had never seen her this bubbly and happy.

"I see that you are in a good mood today," I said.

"Doc, I am on cloud nine."

"What is making you happy today?" I asked. I had an idea, but I wanted to hear it from her.

"Ronald got me a birthday present." She smiled and then put her wrist in my face. She shook the bracelet that she had on in my face. It was a charm bracelet. "Charm bracelets are my favorite." She beamed with pride.

Looking at something that I had paid for involuntarily did not sit right in my stomach. "Excuse

me, I will be right back. I need to use the restroom,"
I said. I didn't even give her a chance to respond
before I got up with my hand on my stomach.

I opened the door to the restroom in my office,
stepped inside, and quickly closed the door behind
me. The rumbling in my stomach caused me to
throw up in the toilet. I was shocked. Her news
had really made me sick to my stomach. I walked
over to the sink and began to rinse off my face and
hands. I looked at myself in the mirror and shook
my head in disgust.

"Get yourself together, Marcus," I coached myself aloud. I grabbed a few paper towels to dry my
face and hands.

When I returned to my seat, I looked directly
at Melissa and said, "I'm sorry. Something I ate
earlier must have upset my stomach." I rubbed my
stomach.

"Yeah, that happens to the best of us," she said
with a faint smile.

"So where were we?" I asked.

"We were talking about Ronald's gift to me. My
new bracelet." She stuck her arm out and jiggled
the bracelet. My stomach lurched again.

"Oh, yes. That looks nice," I said and tried not
to grimace or show my true feelings. "Did he get a
job?"

"I don't know. I just know that he popped up
with it and some roses at my job. All the ladies at

my job want Ronald, but they know that he is all mine." She was smiling proudly. It was like she had forgotten all the previous drama he had put her through.

"All is right in your world now?" I asked. I needed to burst her bubble and give her the reality of the situation.

"Yes, it's all coming together now. Ronald is coming around to the fact that I got his back, and now he is proving his love for me."

"After just one gift?" I asked, prodding her.

"I told you that he has been more affectionate with me lately." Her smile had waned a bit.

"But you said you thought that he was cheating you," I reminded her.

"I was acting foolishly. I thought that he was covering up something. I think I was wrong," she admitted.

"You don't think that he is cheating on you anymore?" I probed.

"It's on the back burner for now. I am going to give him the benefit of the doubt. Us women can be too aggressive when it comes to letting the man care for us."

"Do you still think that you need to come to therapy?" I asked. I needed to get out of this mess. If she was out of the picture, then Ronald would be as well.

"Doc, are you trying to get rid of me?"

"No, Melissa," I said as I looked at her intently. "It seems to me that you have come to a place where you are satisfied with your growth and relationship."

"Doc, that is something that I will think about. I will get back to you on that." Her smile was back on high again.

"There is no pressure. It's just an observation."

"Doc, I know that you have my back. I will keep you posted." She got up and sashayed out of my office.

I hung my head in shame. I was hoping that she would be moving on. I just had to wait and see.

Chapter 28

Evan

I was working with the last client of the day, and I was exhausted. Getting people into shape was an enormous task, but I enjoyed it. I was a results type of guy. It was a natural high for me to see the people I helped succeed. But doing my job and keeping myself in shape at the same time was demanding. And clubbing and partying with my boys also took a lot out of me. Especially the liquor and the hangovers that followed.

I looked at myself in the mirror while my client was busy doing a set of squats, and I noticed that while I was still ripped and tight, I had developed a little bulge of fat on my stomach. I vowed to work out even harder over the next couple of days.

Against my better judgment and my own set rules, I had a man now. The relationship wasn't conventional by my standards. I usually vetted a person before I took a serious approach to them.

Relationships meant a loss of freedom and exploration. I liked them both. I was young and didn't want to settle down. Yet here I was in the middle of a relationship . . . and oddly, I was enjoying it. I would let it flow.

"All right, Luke," I called. "That was a good set. I will see you in a couple of days."

He was a thick white male with a heavy build, but he would be a work of art when I was finished with him. He wasn't attractive to me, and that helped me guide him through his training without lusting after him. I wasn't a total slut. I had some bad behaviors, which I was working on. I was a work in progress.

Once he was gone, I went to the shower room, washed up, and then exited the gym. I just wanted to go home and lie down and binge on some Hulu or something. Something with Vin Diesel in it would rock me right to sleep.

I pulled up to my home and was just about to get out of the car when my phone rang. It was Allen.

"Hello," I said when I answered the call.

"Hey, are you home?" he asked.

"I just pulled up."

"Great. Get dressed. I have a surprise for you. I'm treating you to dinner. I will text you the address."

"Really?" I was surprised but hesitant at the same time. "Where are you taking me?"

"It is a surprise. Try to get to the address in forty minutes."

The phone went dead, and then an address popped up in my text messages. While I really didn't feel like it, I entered my home and then got dressed up to please the masses. I had a few outfits on standby that could set the world on fire.

Following the instructions that the GPS gave me, I headed to the location Allen had sent me. I had a queasy feeling in my stomach, like something major was about to go down, and I just didn't know about it.

The restaurant that I pulled up to looked quite fancy. The patio in front had some outdoor tables and chairs, nice shrubbery, and trellises wrapped in lights.

I exited my car and walked toward the front door. I entered the restaurant and was greeted by an older gentleman at a podium.

"Good evening, sir. Welcome to Edwardo's. How can I help you today?" He was so warm and inviting. He eased the tension that I had going on in my stomach.

"I'm meeting a friend here."

"Ah, yes. I was waiting for your arrival. Follow me this way," he said, and then he stepped from behind the podium.

I followed him through the restaurant, which had lit candles and soft music playing over the sound system. The atmosphere was soothing and calming. There were plenty of couples, and they looked to be enjoying themselves.

We reached the table where Allen was seated, but he was not alone. Two other people shared the table with him. This gave me pause. I was instantly nervous. I did not like surprises. Especially new people. I looked at Allen in the eyes, waiting for an explanation or a clue as to who these people were. I was still on the fence about "us," and here he was pulling off an unsavory surprise. I was furious. I tried to hide it, but I think my face gave me away.

"Hey, baby," he said as he stood up. He stepped over to me and gave me a kiss, which caught me off guard. My anger changed to embarrassment just that fast. Public displays of affection were no-no this early in a relationship.

"Hey." I smiled as I looked at the two other people at the table. They were older looking, maybe in their late forties, early fifties, if I had to take a guess.

I pulled out the only vacant chair at the table. I assumed that it was for me. I felt out of place. I was like a new kid at a new school. I was guarded.

I looked at Allen and then at the other two people at the table. They were smiling at me. I smiled back to be polite. I still wasn't feeling it.

"Mom, Dad, this is Evan. My boyfriend."

He looked at me after he said it, and I just smiled. Hearing it made it real.

Boyfriend. I let that swim around in my head for a few minutes. I wasn't going to tell anyone about this new status that we had. Especially my boys. I mean, they had met him, but he was just a prospect, not a reality, to them. Now he was introducing me to his parents.

This was happening too fast for my comfort. He was on the fast track, and I needed to slow him down. I wasn't going to do it in front of his parents, though. That would be insensitive, and I wasn't trying to hurt his feelings.

"We are so glad to finally meet you. Allen has told us so much about you," the mother said.

"I'm glad to meet you as well," I replied, but I wasn't sure about how sincere I sounded. I like meeting new people, just not under these circumstances. This was like a shotgun introduction.

"My son has never introduced us to any of his other friends," the father said. He smiled after he finished his comment, but I could feel the tension in the word *friends*. This was not his favorite subject.

"Yes, you are the first and only. I hope," Allen said as he put his hand on my shoulder.

"I believe in hope." It was the only thing that I could muster up without sounding like a jerk or saying something foolish. I felt like a fish out of water.

"Aw, isn't that sweet?" the mother gushed, and then she looked over at her husband. She was in love with him, but he was not in this situation. That would make two of us.

"Yes, how . . . sweet." The father looked at me and then at Allen. "My son says that you are a physical trainer. That's how you make a living?" he asked.

"Yes, sir," I answered. "I do very well for myself." I felt like beating my chest like I was a big ape. I was proud of myself and the work that I did. I was not going to let someone try to intimidate me or judge my profession.

He wasn't a physically threatening man. It was his facial expressions that gave me tension. He had either a stern look on his face or a smirk that gave the impression like he was insulted or something.

I felt like he was talking down to me. Allen's parents were dressed very well. Like they had money and a good education. Perhaps that was why I sensed that Allen's father was condescending toward me.

"What do you do for a living?" I asked, turning the spotlight on him.

"I am a college dean." He smiled proudly. His wife beamed with pride.

"Oh, that is admirable. Everyone has their passion. I love mine," I stated.

"Yes, Dad. He is very good at his job. That is one of the things that attracted me to him. He changes lives, just like you do."

I felt some resentment when Allen compared me to his father. Like he was the standard. I loved the beat of my own drum. I didn't march to anyone else's.

This whole scene was making me totally uncomfortable. I regretted all of this. I had a mind to get up and walk out on all of this.

However, my upbringing didn't teach me to walk out on things abruptly. I wasn't a jerk in that sense. And Allen was a nice guy, and I was beginning to enjoy his company. He was putting in a great effort to please me, and I needed to make some adjustments on my part.

The waiter came over just then and greeted us. "Good evening, ladies and gents." He handed us menus. "I'll give you some time to look at those." He left the table.

I looked at Allen and then his parents.

"Evan, order whatever you want. It's all on me," Allen's father announced with a smile or a smirk. I wasn't sure which, because the conversation earlier had me in my feelings, and I could be misreading him because of my emotions. I decided I would play the game and order the most expensive thing on the menu. He had the money, so I would help him spend it. I was hungry too.

We perused the menu in silence, and when it was clear that we were ready to order, the waiter hurried over to our table.

"So what can I get you today?" he asked.

When it was my turn, I ordered caviar with blini as an appetizer and filet mignon as an entrée.

The expression on Allen's father's face was one of surprise. "Those are great choices," he said as he looked at me. "I'm glad my son picked someone with some taste."

I didn't know if that was a shot at me, but I ignored it and simply smiled.

"He chose our son, and I know that is a great choice," Allen's mom chimed in.

It looked to me like Allen's father frowned, but I could be wrong. Maybe I was paranoid or was seeing things. This whole scene was making me crazy. I was losing my mind in an effort to keep up with the father and at the same time not hurt Allen. Even though I hadn't signed up for any of this.

I looked at Allen and then leaned over and kissed him. I was shocked at myself. I kicked myself for going against my rules. I knew that Allen was going to run with this even further.

"Yes, Allen is a great catch. Like father, like son." I grinned at Allen's dad. "I bet he is a chip off the old block."

"You can say that again." Allen's mom playfully nudged her husband.

The night went smoothly after our appetizers were delivered to the table. Allen's father continued to throw some shade, but it was like water off a duck. Meanwhile, I enjoyed the company of his wife and Allen.

Chapter 29

Keith

Kingston was all that I could think about when I was getting dressed to meet him at the party he had invited me to. It had been a minute since I'd gone to a party. I was assuming that this was a company party since he hadn't been specific. I dressed casually. A blazer, jeans, and loafers seemed appropriate. I wanted to impress but not seem stuffy.

I had to impress him and the people who were his higher-ups.

Kingston had texted me the address. I was about forty-five minutes from the location, which was in a rural area that I was not familiar with. So I really didn't know what to expect.

My nervousness about this party took me back to when I was being adopted and the negative feelings that I had about myself at the time. No matter how gifted or talented one was, there was always room for doubt. Intelligence did not equate to confidence. Confidence came from experience. Trial and error. I had zero confidence when I was being adopted.

My adoptive parents understood this, and they tried to instill in me solid values and a sense of self-worth. I was taught to do what it took to get the job done. They said hard work would pay off even if you failed sometimes. And they told me that it was okay to fail, as long as you picked yourself up and tried again.

I was hoping that all that training would pay off soon.

While I drove, I listened to music that soothed me and inspired me. I wanted a drink to take the edge off. I had high expectations of myself and this party. Would I be charming or boring? Would the other guests judge me on my appearance?

The winding roads in my mind and on GPS started meshing, and I swerved on the road a few times because I was wrapped up in my thoughts.

I finally pulled up to a large gated entrance. Once the guard let me through the gate, I made my way up a long driveway to an enormous house. Bright lights illuminated the windows, and you could see people moving about inside.

The fluttering in my stomach grew stronger. I pulled up to the front door, where someone—I assumed he was the valet—was waiting.

I put my car in park and the gentleman walked around to my side of the car. I stepped out from behind the wheel.

"Good day, sir," the valet greeted. "May I have the keys to your car and your cell phone please?"

"My cell phone?" I looked at him in surprise.

"Yes, sir. Phones are not permitted in the building," he stated. "Please turn your phone off and place it in your glove compartment."

I did as I was told. I had experienced this only at a concert before, but I had known beforehand. Suddenly being asked to surrender my phone left me with questions and intensified my nervousness.

After reluctantly stowing my cell in the glove compartment, I walked into what was a well-furnished house. As I was admiring all the great artwork and the nice furniture, I was greeted by a man I did not know. He was a tall white male in a suit and tie.

"You are a guest of Kingston. Follow me this way," he said, his demeanor dry. He turned, and I proceeded to follow him.

He led me into a room where it was just him and me. I could hear music, but it was faint. The doors to the rooms that we had passed were all closed.

"Please have a seat. There is some paperwork that you must sign before you can join the party," he said as he looked at me.

"Paperwork?" I repeated as I sat down. I was sure I looked confused.

"The proprietor of the home has a particular guest who likes particular things, and this guest's privacy is of the utmost importance," he informed me.

He slid a paper toward me. "This is a binding nondisclosure form that will keep your and our fellow guest's privacy safe for the entirety of your participation here."

"I'm lost." I looked at him like he had two heads. "Why would I need to sign something like that for a party?"

"These parties have special guests. And Kingston assured us that you would fit in with these special guests. Was he mistaken?" He looked at me, waiting for me to respond.

I hesitated as I pulled the paper close to me, and then I signed it. I felt totally uncomfortable with the act I had just committed.

We left the small room, and he led me down the hallway to another room. He opened the door, and I entered a room filled with all men. There wasn't a woman in sight. That wasn't a deal breaker. It was just odd. A party with no women? Interesting.

Kingston popped up behind me. "Welcome, Keith. I'm so glad that you could make it."

"Hey, sir." I reached out to shake his hand, but he pulled me into a long embrace instead. It felt like it had the last time. I felt horny. His scent caused me to take in a breath. A long breath.

Then I remembered that this wasn't that type of party.

"I'm so glad that you made it," he said as he pulled away from me. He looked me in the eyes. I looked away after a few seconds.

His firm gaze just did something to me.

"I have some friends that I want you to meet," he said as he put his arm around my shoulder.

He led me around the room. There were white men, Asian men, and a few black men in the mix. I smiled as he walked me up to each man. Kingston didn't give out the men's professional titles or mention their affiliation with the bank. He simply said their names, and they all reached out and pulled me in for a hug. Just like he had when he greeted me. It all felt weird.

One of the men even said, "Good pick," and bumped fists with Kingston.

"What did that guy mean by 'good pick'?" I asked Kingston when we got a moment alone.

"Oh, he is a very important guy in your development. He's always looking for fresh talent." He smiled.

"Oh, okay." I nodded. "Where are the women at this party?" I asked.

"This is an exclusive party. You must be invited. Old boys' club, as they say," he explained. This satisfied me. His explanation made sense.

The music in the room increased in volume suddenly, and then the doors opened and waiters in Speedo briefs came in with trays of wine to serve to the guests.

There was a collective jubilant roar, and then the room became alive with action. The men in the room began to grab both the wine and the waiters. Kissing and fondling were rampant. I was in immediate shock.

"What in the . . ." I stopped short of cussing in front of Kingston, even though I didn't think that anyone would notice.

"You like what you see?" Kingston asked me.

"What is going on in here? What kind of party is this?" I asked.

"It's an exclusive party. Only those who qualify are invited. It's for anyone who wants a push up the corporate ladder." He looked at me in my face. He didn't blink.

Before I could say anything else, I was pulled on by an older male, who then aggressively fondled my body. I pushed him off me and walked toward the door.

Kingston followed me and pulled me to the side of the door to get my attention.

"Is this how you are going to be? I took a chance and brought you to an opportunity to advance your career, and now you are turning your back on me?" His face was close to mine, and I could feel his hot breath. His strong facial features and serious expression let me know that he was not playing.

"I'm not a prostitute," I barked. I had standards.

"Did I say that you were one?"

"No, but that is implied by the activities in this room and the potential advancement of my career."

"Look, Keith. You are a very good-looking guy, and these guys want to appreciate that. There is no sex involved. Just some harmless fun and fantasy."

I looked at him and then around the room, observing the men's activities. I was no prude, but I wasn't this adventurous.

"Just try it one time, and if you don't like it, then you can go about your business, and we can pretend that this never happened," Kingston proposed.

"I need to go home and think about this. Can I do that?"

"Yes. I will talk to the guys and let them know what is going on. You are free to go. I will be in touch."

I exited the room and then building as fast as I could. My car was brought to me.

I quickly climbed behind the wheel, pulled off, and watched the house disappear in my rearview mirror. The winding roads caused me to think about what I had just witnessed behind those walls. I had never been exposed to that type of thing in my life. I was no prude, but I was raised to be a bit reserved. My adoptive parents wouldn't be proud if I chose to engage in the activities Kingston was pushing.

Was my career worth the loss of some of my dignity? Life was all about choices and decisions. I was more confused than ever about my future.

This was not how I had planned my life. The fact that I was even thinking about playing Kingston's games was blowing my mind. I needed a drink. I needed my boys.

Chapter 30

Justin

The music was pumping though the speakers.

The people were on the dance floor.

The drinks were flowing.

My boys and I filled glasses with our choice of liquid love.

I was reminiscing about the date with Marlon a few days ago. I was floating on cloud nine, as they said. I had to admit that I was ready to go all the way with him sexually, but I was glad that we had waited.

It was a mistake that I had made many times before. I had genuinely thought that sex was intimacy. I now knew differently. Getting to know someone mentally and spiritually first was essential to building a lasting relationship.

My boys were my rock. We had been through many bad times and relationships. More than enough to make you scared to try again. Emotional pain was a motivator not to get into anything that may become serious.

I felt different now. Marlon had changed my mind about the possibility of love. I was trying not to become caught up, but it was hard to do. He was treating me so well.

That was why I had convinced the boys to go to the club where he was DJing tonight. I wasn't trying to keep an eye on him . . . but I was. I knew how these clubs could be. Everyone was looking for a good time or a hookup, but not on my watch. I was making my claim.

"Justin, you sure are quiet right now. What's going through that head of yours?" Keith inquired.

"Oh, not much. I'm just enjoying the scenery and my time off from work. I'm ready to let loose."

I pumped my body a little bit to the music, which had some heavy bass in it. I zeroed in on Marlon as he was doing his thing. I saw a few people go up to his booth. This made me a little antsy. I wanted to go up there and monitor his interactions, but that would be crazy.

I had already staked my claim, but we had been dating for only about a month. I had to keep my cool. All of this was still under the radar.

I got up from our table and headed toward the bar to get myself another drink. I swayed my way through the crowd. The people I passed had a look of pleasure and contentment on their faces as they danced. The alcohol that I already consumed had given me a buzz, but I wanted more. I was feeling great.

I got to the bar and ordered my drink. I was jamming to the music and minding my business. Then I heard the person I was standing next to say, "That deejay is a cutie. I wonder if he's available?"

"Baby, don't even waste your time trying to get with him. I heard him turn down a few people tonight. He said he don't poop and eat in the same spot."

"Wow, really? That is too bad. But he's right. He is fine, though." He shook his head in disappointment.

"True, he is very good looking. Whoever gets him is in for a treat," I said and then turned and walked away.

The predator in me was ready to pounce on anyone who looked like they would get in my way. I hated to be this way, but I had to do what I had to do.

I got back to our table and sat back down. I had my eye on Marlon as he continued to do his job.

"Who was that you were talking to at the bar?" Keith asked as he gave me a sly look. Like I was getting ready to sneak off.

"Somebody that wanted all this goodness." I rubbed my hand up and down my body seductively and then laughed.

"Uh . . . so did you give them your number?" Keith asked.

Evan and Marcus looked at me out of curiosity.

"No, he looked like an appetizer, not a main course," I joked.

"Just say that he wasn't worth a trip to the bathroom," Evan joked and laughed. We all fell out laughing.

"Justin, it's been a minute for you. You might want to go get that drop of water for your dessert." Evan laughed.

"I'm not as dry as you think," I shot back.

"So, you out here getting some on the low?" Marcus asked.

"No, my best friend has been handling business." I waved my hand in the air like a tambourine player and chuckled. I had to cover up for my slipup, even though we technically had not had sex.

"Yes, a hand does do a body good," Keith interjected with a laugh.

"Amen," we all chimed in at the same time and then laughed.

This club life, along with the shot of liquid love, did make everyday life easier to manage. I enjoyed feeling the buzz, as did the rest of my boys. We all exited the club at the same time and made sure that we got in our cars safely.

I texted Marlon a kiss emoji before I pulled off. He sent one back, causing me to smile. I was going to sleep well tonight.

Chapter 31

Marcus

I was in my office, contemplating life and choices. I just couldn't get myself together. I was knee-deep in my own poo. I was sick of feeling sorry for myself. I was not incompetent. I just thought with the wrong part of my anatomy, and it had got me in trouble. It would not be the first time and was probably not the last.

I had wanted to tell my boys what was going on so many times, but I was supposed to be the wise one. I had never before put myself in this kind of situation, and I advised against it with my clients and friends.

A drink would be love right now. I needed to escape this nightmare. I cleaned up the office, grabbed my belongings, and headed for the door.

There was a knock on the door before I reached it. I didn't have any more appointments scheduled for today, so I assumed it was someone knocking on the wrong office door.

I waited for the person to go away, and then I would leave. I didn't have any more patience for human contact. I wanted to come in contact with a few drinks and maybe the dance floor.

I waited a few seconds, and the person stopped knocking. I exited my office and immediately halted right outside my door.

"Hey, Doc." Ronald smirked as he greeted me. I was ashamed to say he was looking fine and well groomed. I thought I had paid for the clothes that he had on.

"What can I do for you?" I asked. That was a loaded question, and I needed to rephrase it.

"Well . . ." I could tell that he was relishing the moment.

"I meant, what do you want?" I gave him a serious face so that he couldn't see the lust behind my eyes. I was getting aroused just thinking about our last session.

"We need to talk. In your office." He walked toward me.

"I'm not your therapist."

"I need to talk, and you need to listen. In your office." He pushed past me and turned the knob on my unlocked office door.

I followed behind him and stood in the middle of my floor. I was not about to sit down or get comfortable.

He got right down to business. "I was talking to my other boo, Melissa. She told me about her therapist and how he was trying to get rid of her. Telling her that she was fixed, and she didn't need any more therapy and all that stuff."

"Okay," I said as I looked at him, my expression neutral.

"You know that when I am with her, I really try to tune her out, because she be on some nonsense. Yap . . . yap . . . yap. Just like a little lapdog. But she good in the bed, so I stay around."

"Get to your point, Ronald."

"My point is that *I* will tell you when her therapy is over. Unless you want me to call the people about your license and all that. I mean, what else can you do without your license besides them lips and hips?" He laughed.

I wanted to pick up a vase and throw it at his head, but I was not a victim. I was a willing participant who was getting his just deserts.

"You know that this can't go on forever," I stated.

"I'm an opportunist. I know how to stretch things out. Well, you know all about that too." He grabbed his crotch and squeezed it.

He was a real jerk. A good-looking, well-endowed jerk. I hated him and myself. I hated how weak my flesh was.

I was going to figure out how to get out of this and keep my job. I just needed some time to figure this out.

After he left my office, I followed suit minutes later. When I got outside, I looked back at the building. My livelihood was in this building. My hard work, sweat, and tears had been poured into this building.

My patients needed me, and I needed to be there for them. I just could not give up that easily. One mistake was not going to ruin my life.

I got in my car and started it.

My car drove me to the club by instinct, or at least it seemed that way.

I was a wreck on the inside. But I held my head up high as I opened the door to the establishment and went in.

Nine p.m. was still kind of early for the club, but I didn't care. To my surprise, Evan was sitting at the bar when I walked in. I was really hoping to be by myself in here tonight, but it was what it was.

"It's too early for drinking, isn't it?" I asked Evan as I plopped down in the empty seat beside him.

"Hey, sir. Your car drove you here too." He laughed.

"You right about it." I chuckled back.

"Where are Keith and Justin?" Evan asked.

"I haven't talked to either one of them today, or for a few days, as a matter of fact," I answered.

"Yeah, I have been a bit preoccupied myself too," Evan added.

"Let's worry about them later. I will let these drinks do some work tonight." I signaled the bartender, and he headed in my direction. I ordered my first drink. It arrived within minutes.

"Evan, have you ever done something so stupid that you couldn't even believe it yourself?" I asked as I swirled the ice rocks in my drink. I wasn't going to tell him my business, but I needed some "messy behavior" company right now.

"Marcus, I have too many to count." He nodded his head as he spoke.

"Man, I have all this wisdom and smarts, but I don't use them for myself. I feel like an idiot." I drank some of my drink and then looked around the room in shame. I wondered how many people in this room were trying to drown their sorrows in drinks. I couldn't be the only one.

"Dude, we flesh and blood. Mistakes are inevitable. That's why God blessed us with alcohol. It's to get us to the other side of problems. Or to at least numb us until they go away." Evan gave a laugh.

I smiled, but I was hurting inside. I had thought that this behavior was above me, but clearly, it was not.

"I don't know what you are going through. I do know that you are smart enough to get out of it. That is always how you have been. Sometimes it gets on my nerves, but you are an intelligent mofo. Trust in you. You got this," Evan said reassuringly.

He pulled me in for a hug, and then we enjoyed ourselves for a few hours and went home.

Friends were necessary. I needed my friends, and there was no doubt that they needed me.

Chapter 32

Evan

My bed felt so good right now. I was not a lazy person, but I needed to sleep in today. One of the luxuries of owning your own business was the fact that you could take a break whenever you wanted to take one.

I was a bit hungover from last night, even though Marcus and I hadn't drunk too much. It had been much less than we would normally drink.

Last night at the club, I had just wanted to spend some quality time with myself. I had to take some time for me. I didn't want to see anyone. I didn't even want to look in the mirror to see myself.

I was curious as to what was going on with Marcus. He looked like he had pooped on himself in public and everybody had seen him. He hadn't gone into the details, but it had to be serious. And I hadn't poked or prodded him, because everyone needed time to process stuff in life. He didn't need anyone grilling him. I didn't like it, and I was pretty sure he didn't either.

I rolled around in bed for a few minutes before I hopped in the shower. It was a quick washup, because I was hungry and wanted to fix something to eat. I put on my favorite Mickey Mouse pajamas and matching slippers.

It was a "pampering me" day, and I was going to enjoy it. Solitude was priceless.

I planned on doing some switching in the kitchen.

"Alexa, Play some jazz music."

Music filled the air, and I felt my problems melt away with each passing moment.

I had started prepping my breakfast when my doorbell rang. I didn't have plans for any visitors. This was a me day. I ignored the doorbell and went back to my business. But it rang again and again.

I was not happy. I walked to the door and looked through the peephole. It was Allen, and he had shopping bags. They didn't look like they had food in them.

Flashbacks of the dinner with his parents the other day gave me pause. While I had decided that I would continue to let Allen pursue a relationship with me, his father was a complete turnoff. That was why I didn't do relationships too much: they came with baggage. Mainly family members and their baggage.

Being single meant I had only my own baggage.

Anyway, despite my better judgment, I opened the door. I was curious.

"Hey, baby," he said and smiled as he walked through the door. He kissed me and then kept walking. I could not see what was in the bags.

"Allen, I wanted to spend the day with myself. No company," I said as I followed him.

He proceeded to my living room, where he plopped down on my sofa.

"Woo," he said as he blew out a breath. I thought he was ignoring my last statement.

"Did you hear what I just said?" I gave him a stern look.

"Baby, we have to talk." He looked at me. His face was emotionless.

Was he about to break up with me? That was what his father had convinced him to do, I decided. That was usually what those words meant. Was this my escape from a "relationship"?

Allen was a nice guy, and he was attentive, but he was getting ahead of himself. Especially since I didn't like to be tied down. I didn't want to break his heart. To be honest, he looked like he had some stability issues. He was clingy, and I wasn't a huge fan of that.

"About?" I asked.

"Our future." His facial expression changed. He was smiling now.

It made me nervous.

"Yes, you are so right," I agreed. "We need to talk about—"

"Getting married," he interrupted.

My mouth hung open, and I didn't know what to say. Yes, I did.

"Married?" I looked at him like he was crazy.

"Yes, my parents are going to pay for everything." Excitement filled his eyes.

I started breathing hard. I had not anticipated this. How in the world did he think that we were ready for marriage?

"Married?" I repeated.

"Yes, baby. I got all the magazines here, and we can spend the day preplanning. I already looked at a few venues yesterday and got some estimates. I'm so excited." He spread out the magazines on my coffee table.

"Excited?" I was still stunned.

"Yes, we are going to jump the broom and all that." He bounced on the sofa like a child.

"No . . . no . . . no." I shook my head. "This is not happening. This is too much too fast."

"Baby, we are in love. This is the next logical step. We need to be at one with each other. You don't want that?" He had on a puppy dog face, which normally would melt my heart.

"Not at this moment. I want to know what made you think that after only a few weeks, this was the

next step. Have you lost your mind?" I didn't mean
the last part. I was just angry.

"Lost my mind?" He looked hurt. I regretted
what I'd said. A few tears fell down his face.

"I didn't mean the last part. It is just too much
too fast. We haven't even lived together yet. We
don't really know one another."

"I thought that we could do that as the day approached. I was just trying to keep you happy. I'm
sorry. I was being foolish. I don't want to lose you,"
he said, and then he got up off the sofa.

He walked over to me, then wrapped his arms
around my neck. I didn't stop him, because as I
could see, he didn't take rejection well.

"I need you, and I know that you need me. This
is inevitable. Love is in your face." He leaned in
and gave me a passionate kiss, which I let melt my
tough exterior.

"Listen, let's slow this down," I said, pulling away
from him, trying to get some control back. He was
very persuasive. Or I was very weak. I wasn't sure
which right now.

"You don't want me?" He looked down at the
floor.

"I don't want this pressure. We need to date
more. Learn more." I tried to speak as softly as I
could. I didn't want to hurt his feelings again.

"Pressure is good. It gets the heart going. It
moves us in the right direction. Forward. I'm a

future guy. I want a future with you. I need a future with you. I'm in love with you. I can't live without you," he confessed.

I was not happy with "I can't live without you."

"Allen, you *can* live without me. You did it without me before you met me."

"You don't want me." He backed up. He started trembling.

I walked toward him and pulled him into my chest. He was still trembling. I had never experienced this before.

"I want you . . . to slow down. We can't happen if one is running in front of the other. We need to go at the same speed," I said as I continued to hold him.

I pulled away from him but kept my arms on both of his shoulders. I looked him in the eyes. His eyes were still glossy.

He remained silent.

"Do you understand what I am saying?" I asked him.

"I think so. I just don't want to lose you. I don't want to lose you. I don't know what I would do if I lost you."

"You would live. I am sure of it. I am nobody."

All of this was a turnoff. I felt like I was speeding down a highway and about to have to wreck.

"Allen, let's table this stuff for now. I was fixing breakfast before you came."

"You were?" He smiled.

"Yes. Let me finish, so we can eat and talk some more. I want to get to know you. We can just talk and eat. You know, take it easy," I said as I walked toward the kitchen.

"That sounds nice. I love you. I need you," Allen said as he followed behind me.

He watched me cook our meal. He talked the whole time. I tried to pay attention to what he was saying and to inject some stuff about me in the small talk. I was glad that I had had this talk with him. He now knew where I stood when it came to us. I hoped.

Chapter 33

Keith

I was sitting in my office, trying to focus on work, but I was struggling, since I just didn't want to be here. The urge to go to the club and get something to drink to curb this craziness in my head was strong.

I was trying to avoid people at all costs today. I wanted to call out of work, but that was not something that I did. I toughed it out. I put in the work, and I didn't shy away from a challenge.

The challenge that Kingston had presented to me was different, though. I was in new territory. I wasn't used to compromising. Was what Kingston offering me a real deal?

A knock on the door jarred me from my thoughts.

"Come in," I said against my wishes, since I really wanted to be left alone.

"Hey, boo," Jennifer said as she came into my office. She sat down in one of my chairs, as she usually did.

"How are you today?" I asked, trying to fake enthusiasm. I really didn't have time for playfulness today. My future was at stake. My dignity was on the line.

"My feelings are hurt." She pouted.

"Why?" I asked.

"Kingston has not being paying any attention to me."

"Why do you think that is?" I asked. I knew why now, but she didn't need to know. I didn't think that she could handle the truth. I was still processing it myself.

"I don't know. He talks to me about work, but that is as far as it goes. I mean, I come in here with my best outfits on, which are tight and hug my body, and he doesn't make a pass at me at all. I mean, like, none." She looked at me like I had answers, but I didn't want to provide them. I wanted to tell her she was shaking the wrong tree, but I didn't.

"Maybe he is married," I suggested.

"But he doesn't have on a wedding ring."

"Everyone doesn't have to wear a wedding ring."

"That's crazy." She waved her hand, dismissing my suggestion. "He's probably scared of all this hot fire underneath these clothes."

"That could be it too. You are rocking that outfit." It was true. But it didn't really matter to me. I just wanted to move the conversation closer to its end.

"See? Even you see it, and you are gay. What's wrong with me? I'm hot and fabulous. All day." She laughed.

I just smiled. "Maybe you are trying too hard. Maybe he is waiting to make his move on you, and you keep missing it."

"You know, Keith, that is possible. It could be that I've been too aggressive."

"You know, he may be trying to keep it professional too. He just got here, and his focus may be on work and doing his job," I stated.

"I am so glad that you are in my corner. I don't have to compete with you, and you give out sound advice. You get me to look at the whole picture. I appreciate that."

"That's what friends are for," I reminded her.

"You are absolutely right," she agreed.

Just then, there was another knock on the door.

"Come in," I called out.

It was Kingston. He smiled as he peeked around the door, and then he entered my office.

"Are you busy?" He looked at me and then at Jennifer.

"No. Jennifer and I were talking about work stuff," I lied.

"I'm sorry. Let me get back to my desk." Jennifer got up from her chair and walked past Kingston. When she got past him, she gave him the once-over with her lust-filled eyes.

"Have a great day, Kingston. And you too, Keith."
And with that, she sashayed out of my office.

Kingston closed the door behind her and then
sat down in front of me. "She really has a thing for
me, huh?" he said and smiled.

"Well . . ." I didn't know what to say to that. I was
surprised that he'd even said it.

"You don't have to say a thing. I am a handsome
guy. People like me. I like people liking me." He
laughed.

I didn't know how to respond.

"Don't be shocked. I'm confident, not arrogant.
There is a difference."

"True," I answered.

"My wife scolds me all the time when she sees
women lust over me," he stated.

"Wife?" I asked. I was surprised.

"Yes, sir. I am married, with kids." He crossed
one of his legs over the other. He didn't blink as he
looked at me.

My mouth hung open in surprise.

"Don't be surprised. The parties I go to don't
hurt anyone. I just like to have fun. A different type
of fun."

"So does your wife know about these parties?" I
asked.

"You mean my business meetings?" he answered.
"She knows what I tell her."

"Oh, okay," was all that I could say.

"You know why I am here?" He looked at me.

I wanted to look away, but I didn't. "Yes, I do." I lowered my head.

"I know that it is not an easy decision for you. But I think it will be worth it. These guys just want some eye candy," he stated.

It was just too hard to agree to do this. It was about dignity. My dignity.

"No sex?" I asked.

"No sex," he answered.

"How did you get involved in these parties?" I asked.

"Well, like you, I wasn't moving up the ladder as fast as I wanted to move. I felt stalled, and I needed to make a move. I just didn't know how. Just like I did for you, one of my bosses invited me to a party, and the rest is history."

"You enjoy it?" I asked.

"I already had a taste for it. It takes one to know one. I just needed a push or a pull. Whatever you prefer to call it. I feed my lust this way, and I get to keep my family and my job. A win-win."

I was floored, to say the least.

"I will try it out at least once. What's the harm?" I agreed. I was going against all that I'd been taught. But you only lived once, right? I was feeling crazy for going against the grain. I was curious, and that was what had driven me to agree. I was in control, and I knew that I could handle it.

"True." He smiled. "I'm glad that you will at least try it." He got up from the chair. "Come give me a hug, since I know that is what you like and need."

I didn't hesitate to go around my desk and let him hug me. I was in heaven. His scent and grip sealed the deal for me. I hoped I had made the right decision.

Chapter 34

Justin

Life seemed so good right now. The man of my dreams was a reality, and I was on cloud nine.

I was at one of my clients' houses, doing a home visit. She wasn't an elderly woman, but she was getting on in years. She had fallen and broken one of her hips, and she needed help to get moving again. She also needed help with cleaning her home. She wasn't a slob, but things could get messy when you were recuperating.

She didn't have any children, but she did have family, and they came around to help when they could.

"Judy, how are you feeling today?" I asked as I walked into her living room. It was only the second time that I had been in her home.

She was sitting on the side of a bed that she had in the middle of her living room. It was a temporary situation, so she didn't have to go up and down the stairs.

She had a walker next to the bed so that she could go back and forth to the kitchen and other areas downstairs. She was blessed to have a small bathroom down on the first floor of her row home. She lived close to the inner city of Baltimore.

I wasn't fond of her neighborhood. While I had grown up in the city, I wasn't completely city friendly. I was no punk. I was a believer from a distance. On her block there were guys hanging out on steps and loud music blasting from cars. The drug activity was just about out in the open. I made sure that I didn't leave anything of value in my car. When I walked to her door, I made sure not to smile. A frown could deter some drama. A smile could be misunderstood as a flirtation or a person that was an easy target.

While the crime rate was high, Baltimore had an equal number of good things going for it. Great schools, parks, and blue crabs, to name just a few.

"Justin, baby, this old girl is slow moving. I'm not used to this. I'm used to moving and shaking. Now I am just shaking." She laughed. I laughed too.

"Judy, you will be back popping and locking in no time. Just give it some time," I said, offering some comfort.

"I hope you are right."

"Judy, I have been helping people get back to themselves for a while now. It's not easy, but it is very doable. Trust me." I sat down beside her and patted her hand that was on her knee.

I didn't feel sorry for Judy. She was going to be all right under my care. I knew it.

"You are such a gem." She put her hand on my cheek. "I am glad that you are here. My family helps me out when they can, but it gets lonely in here sometimes."

"Judy, I know all about loneliness. You don't have to be lonely, though. I am here to help you through this. I can't promise you every day, but I will give you my number if you need to talk."

"Baby, you are so sweet. You look like you do not have a problem in the world."

"Judy, I have my share of problems. Everyone does," I said as I looked at her. She had a few gray strands of hair, but not a full head. She looked like she could still snag a few men.

"You look like you have a man that is treating you right," she responded.

I was shocked that she had insinuated that I was gay. I didn't flaunt it, but I lived it.

"Well, I have a friend right now, and he is very good to me. I can't complain." I smiled, just thinking about Marlon. He was a great catch, and with no baggage, from what I could see.

"Justin, keep that man happy, if you know what I mean."

"Yes, ma'am. I will do my best," I said as I got up from my spot beside her. "So, Judy, what do you want to eat?" I asked.

"Cook me one of them TV dinners in there. I'm not hard to please."

"No problem," I said, and I made my way to the kitchen.

It really wasn't a part of my job to cook and clean, but I did it to make the lives of my clients easier.

I had to admit that having a man who cared for me made doing my job a lot easier. It wasn't a drag. I loved it. And that was because I had someone doing for me what I was doing for others. It felt like a wonderful balance to me.

After I heated and served the TV dinner, I continued to spruce up Judy's apartment, and then I helped her with a minor workout. She was already going to therapy a few days a week. I was a maintenance therapist. And I filled in with light home care.

We were at the place to be. The club.

My day hadn't been stressful, but I'd wanted to get out of the house. I just wanted to hang with my boys.

I had a man now, and I was content with my life. At least I thought so. The truth was that I had a negative attitude, which I tried to hide. I was waiting for the bottom to fall out in some area of my life. I tried my best to hide my pessimism, but it seeped out at times.

"If you're happy and you know it, drink your drink," I sang as I lifted my drink in the air with my boys.

We all took a swallow of our different drinks.

"Keith, what's going on with you?" I asked since he was near me in the booth we occupied in the club that we were in tonight. I wasn't really a booth fan. Just in case something popped, I liked to get out of Dodge with the quickness, and booths caused traffic jams.

"I am enjoying my life. Things are good in the neighborhood," he said and then drank more of his drink. He had had more than usual tonight, so I knew that he was lying, but I didn't push the issue, because we were here to leave our problems on the other side of the club door.

"What about you, Evan? Any new, juicy clients?" I asked.

"Nah, not one good looker in the bunch. I'll keep an eye out for one of them for you. Maybe I'll see one you might like," he answered.

"I appreciate that."

"Marcus, what about you? What do you have going on?" I asked.

"Just work, work, work. Listening to other people's problems and getting paid well for it. That's it. Pretty boring life." He shrugged his shoulders and then drank more of his drink. He, too, was drinking more than normal.

"Well, I got a new client, and this lady is hilarious. She is keeping me on my toes," I announced.

"You look happier than usual, though. New clients don't do that to you usually. What's up with that?" Evan said.

"Y'all know that I love my job. Caring for people makes my life meaningful. There is no extra going on," I answered back.

They all looked at me for a moment and then burst into a fit of laughter.

"If you are hiding your fresh meat, just say that. We know that you need you a fresh piece the most anyway," Marcus joked.

I looked at him for a few seconds like I was offended, but then I laughed with him and my other boys.

"Well, I do have someone sniffing around the front door, but he has not broken ground," I declared, a grin on my face.

"Sure, you right!" Marcus said, skepticism lacing his tone.

"Yep, look at those greased-up lips. Them things had some contact with something," Evan said and then laughed.

Keith eyed me down. "They are a little bit shinier than normal."

I didn't like to be the center of attention like this. "Just lip-to-lip service. Nothing else. So, leave it alone." I twisted in my seat, which let them know that I was not feeling the pressure that they were giving me.

"Cool it, y'all," Keith said. "We are making him uncomfortable."

"Thanks," I said as I looked at Keith.

They all moved on, but I was still feeling some type of way, even though they were my friends, and they were just looking out for me. Sometimes they made me feel like the weak or vulnerable one in the group. Like I needed to be protected all the time. I had to stop being so sensitive and enjoy my night.

That was exactly what I did too. I got up out of my chair and went into the crowd to dance and sweat up my clothes. And soon that was what happened. I danced, then drank and gossiped a bit with my boys before we all went home.

Chapter 35

Marcus

My mind was all over the place as I made my way into the building where my office was located. All I could think of was losing my practice and my friends finding out what was going on in my life. That would be so embarrassing, and I didn't want to disappoint them or myself.

I smiled and greeted the usual people, but it was all robotic. I would usually stop and talk to the receptionist. We would laugh and joke. Get a little gossip in. And then I would make my way to my office. None of that happened today. It was all about consequences to me. I couldn't think about anything else. In my mind, I was wondering if this would be one of the last times I walked through those doors.

I had lied to my boys the other night and had acted as if I had everything under control, because I was that one friend who had all the answers except when the issue pertained to myself. I was a therapist who needed a therapist right now.

I made my way to the elevator, stepped on, and as the doors closed, I felt like a door in my life was being closed. I got off on the floor where my office was situated, and slowly walked down the hall. I hadn't paid attention to the artwork on the walls until now. That was odd to me. I couldn't believe that it took a bad decision of my own to slow me down and make me pay attention to the simple things.

I opened the door to my office and cut the lights on.

I looked at my diplomas on the wall and remembered just how long it had taken me to get those and the sacrifices that I had made to earn them. As I looked at them now, I wondered if they were going to be trash soon.

A day or two ago I had received an appointment request from Melissa, and I had granted her one for today. I was so uneasy about this appointment, I couldn't even eat like I was used to over the past few days. One mistake and this was what was happening.

I didn't have a problem drinking and clubbing, though. In fact, I was drinking more lately. Today I was a little hungover from the drinks I had had in the club.

I spruced up the office a bit, because I had neglected that too. I had left files and notes on my desk; I put them away. Some of the plants I had needed tending to. And I needed to replace the plug-in air fresheners.

I could really use a hug right now, someone to let me know that everything was going to be okay, without my having to explain anything.

My first appointment would be here at any moment, and I had to gather the notes for the session.

My first appointment came, and it went. It was a guy going through a midlife crisis, and I almost started to ask him what I should do in my situation, but that would have been crazy.

There was a fifteen-minute break in between my sessions, so I made me a cup of coffee to get me over the hump. I needed a jump start. I stared out the office window, trying to get my mind right, as I sipped my coffee. I needed to tap into my wisdom and get out of this mess.

A knock on the door brought me back to the present. I walked to the door and opened it. Melissa was on the other side, with a bright smile on her face.

"Good day, young lady," I said and then stepped back so that she could come into the room. I didn't mean it. It was just an act. I didn't want to see her or Ronald ever again.

"How are you doing today?" I asked as I closed my door and followed behind her. She took her normal seat before she answered.

"Doc, I think I am doing great."

"Think?" I asked as I sat down. I grabbed the notes from her last session and began a fresh page.

"Well, I was talking to Ronald about giving up the sessions because I thought that I was good in life right now. But he said that there still may be some work to do in my life."

"Oh, okay. How do you feel about that?" I asked.

"At first, I thought that he was calling me crazy." She chuckled and then continued. "But then he said that my mental state and character were stronger than he had ever seen them. He said that it was causing him to be a better mate."

"Okay. That is interesting." I nodded my head.

I was amazed at the determination of this guy. He was going to try to milk this thing for as long as he could.

"Melissa, what are your feelings about Ronald now?"

"What do you mean?" she asked.

"Do you have any trust issues still?"

"Trust issues?"

"Yes. Do you trust him again?" I asked.

"As of late, he has not given me a reason to distrust him." She looked confident in her answer.

"Melissa, that was a yes or no question. You can't avoid answering." I reminded her of things that we had gone over in another session.

"Yes, I trust him." Her countenance had changed. There was a little bit of an attitude with her answer.

"Okay," I said and then made some notes in her file.

"Do you trust *you*?" I asked.

"What?" She looked confused.

"Do you trust the decisions that you make for your life?"

"Yes," she answered.

"Is Ronald a good choice?"

"Yes. I love him."

"You do know that someone can be your choice, but you may not necessarily be *their* choice."

"You lost me," she said.

"We know that Ronald is your choice in a mate, but are you Ronald's choice or an option for him?"

"He loves me." She folded her arms in front of her chest. I could tell that she was not happy right now.

"What would you do if you found out that Ronald was seeing someone else right now?" I asked.

"He's not cheating on me."

"You didn't answer the question," I told her.

"Let's just say things would get ugly. Real ugly. I'm not one to play with." Her leg was crossed on top of the other, and it was bouncing fast.

"I think that you need to evaluate your relationship with Ronald. I can't and won't tell you what to do, but I would think about it if I were you."

"That is not something that I have to think about. I trust me and him. That's all there is to it."

"No problem. You did great today," I assured her.

I was hoping that I had planted enough seeds of doubt in her head for her to let this bum go. For her and for me.

Chapter 36

Evan

It was a Saturday, and I was going to try to break it off with Allen today. I had had plenty of time to drink and think. Drink and think. They said that alcohol was liquid courage, and I needed plenty of both.

The more I'd drunk, the more I'd amped myself up to get rid of this guy. I did not hate him. In fact, he was a great guy, with a couple of flaws. The relationship was just too much pressure, and I felt like he would not slow down. I needed to slow down. While I liked him, I didn't really know him, and he didn't know me. I didn't want either of us to get hurt. I had had a broken heart before; it was not fun.

I was at the restaurant, sitting at a table, waiting for him to arrive. I had to admit that I was nervous about this situation. I didn't know what I was going to say to him to get him out of my hair.

After about ten minutes, I watched him walk through the door of the restaurant. I was floored to see that he was not alone. The person who was with him made no sense. I hadn't told him that this was an intimate date, so I had only myself to blame. They made their way over to the table.

"Hey, guys," I said as I stood up, greeting both Allen and his father. Yes, his father. I couldn't believe it.

"Hey, baby." Allen smiled as he kissed me.

I shook his father's hand longer than I would have liked.

We all sat down, with Allen close to me and his father across from me.

I couldn't believe it. I couldn't believe he had invited his father without asking me or warning me. Obviously, he didn't remember how his father had treated me the last time. Maybe he was oblivious to his father's bad behavior since he was probably this way all the time.

"Oh, Mom couldn't make it. She's not feeling well," Allen informed me.

"Oh, I'm sorry to hear that."

"How are you doing, Evan?" his father asked.

"I am well," I lied.

"My son can't stop talking about you." I wouldn't say he smiled, but it was close.

"Oh, really?" I looked over at Allen and smiled. I had to admit that I loved how he loved on me.

"He speaks very highly of your skill set in your chosen vocation. So, I need to apologize for the last meeting. I was coarse with you, before getting to know you personally. My son suggested that I come with him and get to know you better."

"I accept your apology. I look forward to getting to know you too."

Even though I had said what I said, I still wanted out. This little get-together was more proof than I needed.

"With that being said, I will leave you guys to get to know each other better." Allen stood up from his chair and kissed me goodbye before I could say anything. I wanted to yell at Allen to come back to the table. I was pissed.

I sat there, with no idea about what to say to this man.

"How long have you been working with people?" he asked.

"A little over ten years," I answered.

"That's good." He nodded his head.

Before he could ask me another question, I motioned for the waiter so that I could get a drink to get me through this unplanned event.

"Do you have a drinking problem?" Allen's father asked after the waiter had taken my order. That was a bold question. Who asked these questions?

"No, I don't have a problem drinking." I laughed.

If I was going to be here, I wasn't going to be dry as dust. I was going to be myself.

He nodded his head. "That was actually funny." And then he laughed. "I guess that is why my son is so attached to you."

"I guess so." I shrugged my shoulders.

"Evan, my son can be quite clingy, pushy, and a bit weird."

"Well, it's not too bad," I lied. Even though I agreed with his assessment. However, I didn't know this man. He could be ready to beat me up if I said something harsh about his son. I was going to save my criticism of his son for his son.

"Don't hold your tongue for my boy because I'm here."

"No, sir, I was being honest," I lied again.

The waiter came and brought me my drink, and as the waiter headed away from our table, Allen's father called to him, asking him to bring some shots of Hennessy with a side of vodka. I was shocked. He didn't seem like the type to drink. He seemed conservative to me.

It didn't take long for the waiter to come back with his drink, and then we ordered something to eat. Allen's father ordered another drink before the food came, and he was getting a buzz for sure. He was loosening up and smiling more. I relaxed.

But then he leaned across the table and asked, "Are you bending my son over, or is he bending you over?"

Even though no one had heard him, I was shocked at his question. That wasn't a regular question for a father to ask. Or any man, for that matter.

"I'm what you call the top, sir," I answered in a hushed tone.

"You are built well, so you must be giving it to him well."

I was speechless. I was amazed at what drinks could do to a person.

"Don't be shy, son. I know that you must be doing something right for Allen to want to marry you."

"I'm not comfortable with this line of questions," I said.

"Son, I've seen and experienced much. I played on both sides of the fence too. Everyone has their secrets. My secrets have secrets." He laughed, but I was even more shocked now.

I thought that my soul left my body. I couldn't believe what I was hearing.

Then I felt a foot on my calf. I quickly moved my leg back and looked across the table in shock.

"I think I need some training too." He looked me in the eyes. There was pure lust in his gaze.

"Sir, that is not going to happen," I insisted.

"Nobody turns me down." He looked at me intently.

"Well, I just did."

"My son isn't good enough for you. You need some serious experience. I don't want a commitment like my son. I have a commitment, his mother. I want some fun." He drank more from his drink and then looked at me in the eyes.

"I'm not that person. I can't date a father and a son," I said.

"You don't have to. Dump my son."

I looked at him in shock. I looked around the restaurant again. It felt like I was in the twilight zone. It had to be a dream.

"Sir, I am not that heartless. I can't dump your son for you. How could you suggest that?"

"Then I will dump him for you. No problem." He swallowed the last of his drink.

"No, sir. I can't let you do that."

"Why? You don't love him. I can tell that because you are continuing this conversation. Someone not interested would have walked out and left me at the table. Something tells me that the manhood between your legs thinks quite a bit for you, and now is no different. So, I'll get rid of your problem, and you will handle mine."

I just nodded my head in shame, because I felt lower than scum. Yet I was relieved.

"I'll get your number from my boy, and then you can start getting me into shape."

Our food arrived, but I didn't have an appetite for food. I needed another drink and a spine.

Chapter 37

Keith

I found myself in my car and once again in front of the house that Kingston had invited me to for a party.

I wasn't the only one to arrive. Valets were helping others with their cars. It was all men and no women.

Again, I was nervous out of my mind. I was sweating under my clothes, and I could not stop fidgeting.

I couldn't believe that I had agreed to do this. I was a person who had established my *nevers* and *evers* a long time ago. I was going to work my way to the top with integrity and no shortcuts. However, here I was compromising my integrity for a climb up the ladder.

I looked at myself in the rearview mirror. I smiled and tried to get myself into a better mood. I didn't know what to expect. I just knew that I didn't have to have sex with anyone.

The routine was the same as the last time. I left my phone in the car, and the valet parked it.

I entered the house, stepping into the foyer. This time I was escorted to a room with an envelope on the door. It had my name on it.

I hesitantly took the envelope and opened. I read the note inside it.

> Welcome to "the show." This is a hands-off event. Just look and enjoy. Feel free to enjoy the show. You are invited to pleasure yourself, but please clean up after yourself.
>
> Enter the room. Your assigned seat is in the middle of the room. Again, enjoy and keep your hands to yourself.

I did as I was instructed.

My assigned seat was a nice plush chair with a small table beside it. I sat down in the chair and stared at the bottle of lubricant on the table. There was also hand sanitizer and washcloths along with it.

There was no way that I was participating in any sexual acts on myself here. I was hoping that I could make it out of here with my pride and sanity intact.

This was something that I would suppress, pushing it into the recesses of my mind.

There was a huge king-sized bed in the room that looked soft and luxurious. I was tempted to roll around in it. The whole room felt like money had been well spent on it. They had room-darkening curtains, and the walls had been painted a dark color. It was like they didn't want any light in the space except for that from the candles that had been placed around the room.

There were two doors on both sides of the bed. I was curious about what was going on behind them, but I sat where I was in anticipation.

Soon soft music began to play, and then the first door opened. My heart raced in my chest as if I were a participant in a game show. Not long after, a man in a cat costume came out. He crawled onto the bed and then wagged his tail. He raised one of his hands and then licked it, as if he was about to start grooming himself.

He rolled around on the bed and lay on his back. I felt weird just watching this show. I was so glad that there were no other people in the room. I knew there were people that really liked this stuff, but I wasn't one of them.

Then the second door opened. Another guy came out, and he was dressed in leather attire, with a leash dragging behind him.

The guy in the catsuit rolled on to his "legs" and began to get excited. The guy in the leather suit walked up to the bed and stuck his hand out in front of the cat. The cat began to lick his hand and up his arm. The leather man began to moan in pleasure.

I didn't realize it, but I was becoming aroused. I was shocked. Then the leather man released his manhood from his pants, and the cat began to "clean" him. The leather man rubbed the cat's behind like a human would do to a real cat.

It didn't take long for the two to end up naked and in the bed. The cat was an older male, and the leather man a young male, probably around my age.

They began to get it in, and I gave into the heat in the room and pleased myself.

I relieved myself and looked on as they finished. The cat began to "clean up" the leather man.

They exited the room as easily as they had come in. I sat in the chair, feeling a minor sense of shame. I cleaned myself up with the things on the table.

I exited the room. There was a guy standing outside the room when I got into the hallway.

"We hope that you enjoyed yourself," he said.

I nodded my head. I really didn't have words for anyone right now. I just walked down the stairs and to the doorway so that I could go home and really clean myself up.

I was feeling really icky all over my body and in my mind. I was keeping this act to myself.

As soon as I got into my house, I showered and then had myself a few drinks. I had to try to drink away the shame. If I could.

Chapter 38

Justin

The police sirens were blaring down the street and were followed by ambulance sirens going off. I looked around the block I was on and then got out of my car. Normally, I would be on high alert, but today I was a low alert. I guessed fresh love would do that to you. I had love for everybody right now.

I made my way up to Judy's porch. Knocked on the door and then opened it. She knew what time I was coming, and the door was usually unlocked for me.

"Hey, Judy, Judy," I said in a singsong way. It was a Friday, and the weekend was calling me. I could not wait to spend time with my Marlon and my boys. Separately, of course.

She was posted up on her couch, as usual, and she gave me a bright smile as I walked up to her.

"Hey, sunshine," she greeted me. "You are looking very sexy right now. Who are you prepping for?"

"Oh, I'm hitting up a club tonight with my boys, and maybe I'll have some fun with my boo this weekend too," I said as I sat down beside her. "What have you been up to?" I asked her.

"Baby, I been getting older by the minute." She laughed.

"That's all of us," I replied.

"Chile, I woke up with something new aching."

"What is that?" I asked.

"My kitty kat been aching." She laughed.

"Judy!" I looked at her and blushed.

"Justin, you are young and may not have experienced it yet, but everyone gets a turn. Everyone needs some attention down below. My furnace flame is not out. It's just low."

We both laughed and fell into each other.

Soon I got up and started to spruce up her home. She wasn't a messy person, but she did need the help that I offered.

Judy was preoccupied with watching *Judge Judy*, while I completed some tasks around her house. I cleaned up the kitchen and the small bathroom that was on the first floor, then threw a load of clothes in the laundry for her. I also prepared her a small snack.

I had just brought her the snack that I prepared when there was a knock on the front door. I looked at the door, waiting for Judy to give me instructions. I didn't open people's doors unless I was instructed to do so.

"That's my niece," Judy told me. "Can you open the door?"

I walked over to the door and opened it. This beautiful brown-skinned woman stood on the other side of the door. She had a little girl with her, and she was cute as a button.

I stepped back away from the door and let them walk in. The little girl automatically ran to Judy. Judy squeezed her in a tight hug.

"Hi, Lisa. How my baby been?" Judy asked the little girl.

"I've been a good girl," she answered.

I stood by as I watched Judy's grandniece interact with her.

"Angela, how are you doing?" Judy asked as her niece sat down on the other end of the couch.

"Auntie, I am going to be okay," she answered. "I have some rough days."

"You will get over that bum," Judy offered.

"Auntie, you make it sound so easy."

"I'm still confused on how a man can have a wife and child and then all of a sudden say he is attracted to men."

"Auntie!" She tried to cover up her daughter's ears, but I thought that it was too late.

"I'm just saying. I'm lost. Wouldn't someone know that earlier in life, Justin?" She looked at me like I was a gay guru.

"I don't know about that. Everyone's story is different. It's not a perfect science," I informed Judy.

"Lisa, go in the kitchen for a few minutes while we talk," her mother instructed her.

The little girl skipped in the direction of the kitchen.

"Have you seen him lately?" Judy asked her niece once Lisa was out of sight.

"We have talked on the phone," she answered.

"It better have been about why your kitty kat wasn't enough. Or his daughter." Judy was off the hook.

"Auntie, it's been only a few months. We both still need time to work through this mess." She wiped a few tears from her eyes.

I had to admit that her pain was coming through so strong that it made me emotional.

"Is your divorce finalized?" Judy asked.

"No, we must wait longer, to try therapy. But he doesn't want therapy. I think that he is already in a relationship and has moved on," Angela revealed.

"What?" Judy yelled.

"I'm not sure. It's just speculation, now. I don't have the heart to ask him. I think it would hurt too bad for him to be truthful with me."

"I just can't believe it. I thought y'all were happy. It's such a shame." Judy shook her head.

"I am still in disbelief too, Auntie." Angela just lowered her head and put her face in her hands. She sobbed long and hard.

I looked around and grabbed a tissue so that she could dry her eyes. I handed her the tissue and watched her dry her face.

"I can't believe that Marlon would treat us like that," Angela commented when she'd wiped away her tears.

Everything in me tensed up. The mere mention of the name Marlon gave me pause. I was sure that she wasn't talking about my Marlon. There were probably thousands of Marlons in Baltimore.

"I mean, I held him down while he chased his deejay dreams. Now he gone, and I am left with a child and a broken heart," Angela went on.

I was standing in the room, but my mind was gone. I mean, this was a lot to hear at one time and by surprise.

I didn't have all the facts, and there could be two Marlons who were DJs. It was possible. I thought.

"Honey, are you all right?" Judy asked me, a look of concern on her face.

"Yes, ma'am." I nodded my head. "I just need to use the bathroom."

I hustled my way into the hall bathroom and closed the door behind me. The fact that I was rattled was an understatement. I didn't want to overreact, however, because this could just be a big mix-up. I had to play it cool and get out of here. I really needed a drink now. I needed enough to drown myself.

I hoped that I was wrong, but I didn't want to be naive about this either.

I looked in the mirror. I was already wearing my worry. I ran the water and then splashed some on my face. "Get yourself together," I ordered myself aloud.

I still had the rest of my shift to finish. I needed my money, and I didn't want to let this news mess that up. I was a big boy, and I was going to act like it. At least until I left here.

I exited the bathroom and continued to do my duties. I listened to Judy and her niece continue to talk about various other things. I was on autopilot and had tunnel vision for the rest of my shift. I smiled and laughed at them at the appropriate times, but it was all fake. I just wanted to get out of there so that I could breathe.

I finally finished my work and exited Judy's house. I sat in my car for a few minutes and then pulled off.

I needed a drink now, and I made my way home to hit up my stash and start my party night early.

Chapter 39

Marcus

My boys and I were all out tonight. I was so glad to be here at the club, and I had already started my night at home. This stress in my life was pulling me here: the club and I were like two magnets connecting.

I looked around the table and saw that my friends were all nursing their drinks. No one was talking, and it bugged me to the core.

"Are we just going to sit here and nurse these drinks?" I asked no one in particular.

There was still silence. I was not going to let my troubles get the best of me. Yes, I was scared as hell and thought about my livelihood quite a bit. But I had come here to forget about that. I had come here to let it all hang out. To escape my problems.

Justin spoke first. "I'm good. I just got a lot on my mind."

"Man trouble?" Evan chimed in.

"Well, I'm not sure about that. I just have a ton of questions that need answers, but they are mainly for myself," Justin said. He looked so low. I felt his pain.

"I hear that," I replied. "I'm doing some self-evaluation as well. Making good decisions is not easy. Even when you have wisdom," I added as I swirled my drink in my hand and the ice hit the sides of the glass. I had my drinks on the rocks, which was just how I felt right now.

I looked over at Evan, and he wasn't dressed to the nines tonight. "Evan, what do you have going?" I asked.

"The same as you all. Bad decisions. I'm good, though. I got it under control." He nodded his head. I didn't believe it, though. He was usually the one of us who was on the dance floor, bumping and grinding on any willing person. He didn't look a mess, but he wasn't behaving normally.

"Keith, you look good. No bad decisions?" Justin asked.

"None that I can think of. I'm just pushing toward my goals. I'm moving in the right direction. I am getting ready to move on up." He smiled.

"That sounds good," I said, but I had my doubts.

"We need to get up and go on the dance floor," I told my boys. "I want to shake off all my problems. The night is young, and so are we."

As if on cue, Beyoncé's "Cuff It" roared through the speakers, causing a mob to hit the dance floor. We joined in the excitement, and I danced like my heart depended on it. I really needed to let loose, and this was perfect.

Song after song came on, and we continued to let loose. Sweat poured from my body, because I had something to prove. I wasn't going to let this situation with Melissa and Ronald beat me. I had overcome too much to let this get the best of me. And looking at my friends, I decided that they probably felt the same way that I did.

We were conquerors, and we were going to beat all our problems . . . I hoped. Since none of us were disclosing our problems, I really couldn't talk about the others. It was mainly speaking through hope right now. I was praying for them and hoping that they were doing the same for me.

We all ended up back at the table and had another round of drinks, which would temporarily erase the pressure we felt from our bad decisions.

I ended up getting an Uber home, because I had drunk too much to go home on my own. That ended up being all our stories. Uber made some money that night off all our drinking and partying.

When I got home, I was still feeling heavy. I ended up hitting up my drink stash. I needed to hug this bottle tonight. I turned on some old-school R & B and let the music drift throughout the house. I swayed to "Angel," by Anita Baker, and let her take me to a place of euphoria. I poured glass after glass of wine, until I was singing full blast with each record that played. Some tears fell as I was filled with happiness.

I woke up hungover on my couch, with two bottles of wine on the table in front of me. I had missed a text message from Ronald.

I read the text out loud. "Hey, boo. Wassup?"

My head was spinning, and I could barely put my feet on the floor. I still had my clothes on from last night. That was a big no-no for me. I was a stickler for cleanliness. I guessed I just didn't care about that last night.

I didn't want to respond to the text, but I did.

I texted back, We need to talk.

He responded with, About?

I replied, Face-to-face.

I texted him the details.

He responded back with, Okay.

Chapter 40

Evan

The Sunday morning sun hit me in my face as I lay in my bed. I was still hungover from Friday. I couldn't face the world today. I canceled all my appointments, because I just wasn't up to working with anyone. For work on Sundays, I collected overtime pay, but I just didn't care right now. I was all about self-preservation.

I got up and showered. I walked around my apartment naked, just as I liked it. I felt so free, even though my decisions had me bound up like a bad bout of constipation.

I still couldn't believe that I had gone from one problem to two. Father and son. *Who does that?*

I looked at myself in one of the floor-length mirrors. My body was toned and looking great. I then grabbed my manhood and shook it in displeasure.

"All this trouble is because of you," I snapped, chastising it.

Truth was, I knew that I had thought with the wrong head too many times.

These results were due to my not respecting consequences. I had gambled and lost control of the situation. I knew now that control was truly a delusion.

I was feeling remorseful, but it was too late for that now. I had to figure out a way out of this situation.

My doorbell rang, letting me know that someone was at the door. I had an idea about who it was, but I didn't want to answer the door.

I went into my room and grabbed a robe. I slowly walked to the front door, hoping that Allen would disappear. But I knew better than that.

I opened the door, and just as I thought, Allen was on the other side of it. His eyes were red and puffy.

"Hey, baby," he said softly.

"Hey," I said back.

"Can I come in?" he asked.

I backed up and reluctantly let him in. I followed him as he walked into the living room and flopped onto the sofa.

I sat on the sofa, just a cushion away from Allen. "What's going on?" I asked. I didn't want to ask, but I had to be hospitable.

"I missed you. You had your phone off yesterday, and I thought that you were dead or something." He looked sincere.

"I was going through something, and I decided to turn my phone off. I apologize that I forgot to let you know. It wasn't intentional. I just needed a break from the world. It wasn't personal." I looked at him intently.

"I'm glad, because I can't live without you. You are my man, and I love you."

He scooted closer to me and kissed me on the lips. I had to admit that his lips were soft and instantly put me in the mood. I had to adjust my robe so that he wouldn't notice my growing manhood.

"I love you too." I almost whispered it. I loved what he did for me. I thought that was equivalent to love.

"You know that my parents love you too," he told me and instantly perked up.

"Really?" I asked.

"Yes, sir. My mother was sold at the first meeting. She said that you have a very nice personality and you are a great catch."

"That's nice." I nodded my head.

"Now, my dad I had to work on. He is such a tough guy. That's why I had to stage a playdate for you guys. I thought it would be great if you guys could bond if you were left alone. I hope it worked."

He looked at me with hope in his eyes. I didn't really know what he expected me to say. I didn't know what his father had said to him about our agreement. I had to assume that he had said nothing about it.

"First, I must admit I was a bit angry at you for not discussing this with me. I don't like those types of surprises. I didn't feel comfortable with the way that your father quizzed me during our first meeting," I admitted.

"I'm sorry. I didn't think that it would be a problem. You have never displayed any anger toward me. And it seems like you know how to handle pressure with the job that you do. Creating results in others takes a bit of pressure, and you do it so well." The sincerity in his eyes let me know that his intentions had been heartfelt.

"I'm not mad at you. I just have a preference to be asked first."

"My father didn't say anything to me about the evening. How did it go?" he replied.

"You and your father have a lot in common."

"What do you mean by that?" he asked.

"You both have strong wills and like what you like."

"True." Allen smiled. I could tell that he was clueless about his father's true nature.

"You have similar tastes in many things. Food, among other things," I said.

"Do you think he likes you?" Allen asked.

"I think so," I answered.

"While I love my father, he can be hard to please at times. I think that is where we are different. I love to please people. I think my father is more of a taker."

"Really?" I asked.

"Yes. My mother waits on him hand and foot. And sometimes he doesn't talk to her the nicest. He can be very demanding. My mother seems to like it, but I think that she is just conditioned to accept it."

"Conditioned?" I asked.

"Yes, she is so sweet and kind. My father has a military background, and she just falls in line. I don't think that my father respects her."

"Oh, wow," I said.

"I don't hate either one for their stance in their marriage. I just know that I don't want that for my own. I want it to be balanced for us. Give and take." He smiled after he spoke.

I was listening to him talk, but my mind kept wandering back to his father and the pact that we had made. I felt guilty, but I had to let this situation play out so that I could be free of them both. Finding out that this whole family—and especially father and son—had some dysfunction didn't make any of this easy. It was amazing how one sexual encounter and some attention had got me into this spot.

I had to fake it until I got out. I cared for Allen, but he had his foot on the gas pedal. I didn't want to gaslight him, but I had no choice but to play chess. I just wanted to make the right moves and get out of this.

"I think that my father likes you, because he didn't say anything to me about you when I last saw him. He didn't say a thing. With him, silence is acceptance."

"I'm glad to hear that. I like that," I admitted. I was being sincere. Everyone liked to be liked. It was human nature. Even though I knew that what his father "liked" was far from me. He liked "it."

"Baby, I am so glad that we got to have this talk. It makes me feel so close to you," Allen gushed as he moved closer to me. His hand made its way onto my leg.

I tensed up a bit and held his hand in place, because I didn't want to give in to his sexual advance. But I was weak.

"Can I?" he said as he pushed his hand beneath my robe. My nakedness underneath my robe didn't help me.

I became aroused, even though I didn't want to do anything sexual. Then I gave in.

He leaned over and began to lick my chest while massaging my manhood. I didn't need help getting it up, but his warm hand was a great stimulant.

Before I knew it, he was on his knees in front of me. My head fell back as he and I enjoyed the pleasure between us.

"You like?" he asked me.

I quietly nodded my head as he continued to work his magic. Guilt floated into my thoughts, but pleasure was overriding my judgment.

The session continued with Allen undressing and pulling a condom from his wallet.

Did he plan this? Was I that predictable?

Was I easy? Who was really in control in this "situationship"?

These were the questions that I had as I strapped up and continued the task at hand.

I was not helping myself by partaking in this pleasure.

I gave him the best that I had, though, and he received it. Then we finished up, and then we cleaned up. Afterward, I walked Allen to the door with mixed emotions.

"Thank you for the love," he said as he turned toward me. He put his arms around my neck and kissed me hard on the lips. When he pulled back, he said, "We were made for each other. I can't wait to spend the rest of my life with you."

I didn't say anything, because I didn't have anything to say. He opened the door and walked out with more pep than he had walked in with.

I closed the door behind him and immediately went to get a drink of liquor. I was steadily digging a hole, one that I didn't know how to get out of.

Chapter 41

Keith

"I am so proud of you," Kingston said as he sat across the table from me. We were out dining at his request. This was what he called a business meeting. I was here to find out when I was getting my promotion. I had done what he asked of me, and I didn't want to do it anymore. I wanted what was due me.

"Thanks," was all that I could muster up. I wanted this to be over and done with.

"How did you like it?" he asked with a bright smile. I didn't feel his sentiments.

"It was different," I answered. The fresh memories flooded my mind. Even though I did enjoy myself, it was not something that I wanted to do again. I wasn't going to tell him that I enjoyed it.

"I watched the tape of the show and saw that you helped yourself to some personal pleasure." He grinned.

"That was just natural instinct," I countered. "It was arousing." I was surprised to learn that they were taping these sessions. I wondered if the tapes were being passed around in the private circle of these freaks.

"I believe that you enjoyed it, and you are being shy right now."

"Well, that is debatable, but it is something that I do not want to do again. I believe that you told me that if I wanted out, I would have my wish. One and done." I sat back, with a smug look on my face.

"Yes, that was what I said, but your actions during your event spoke volumes."

"How so?" I asked.

"If you don't like something, you don't pleasure yourself during the event. A turnoff is a turnoff. A turn-on is a turn-on."

"I disagree," I responded.

"The proof is in the pudding . . . or the video." He laughed.

"Kingston, I am not comfortable doing any of that anymore. When can I expect my promotion?"

"One and done means that you will not get a promotion. You must do your due diligence to move on up."

"I don't like games, Kingston," I said angrily.

"I don't play them. I am a direct person, and I speak carefully. It's apparent that you don't know how to speak up. Or the art of the deal."

I looked at him for a few seconds while I got my thoughts together. I had not expected him to act like this. But I was being gullible and naive if I thought that this guy had my best interests at heart. He was a scout looking for talent, the kind of talent that I didn't know I had. The talent to think I could skip steps on the ladder and it would not cost me anything. I felt foolish and stupid.

"This is what it has come to?" I asked.

"What do you mean?" he asked.

"I guess I am now at your mercy. Your beck and call." I looked at him in disgust. I was madder at myself than at him.

"I'm not that person. I believe in being fair, but I will push the envelope to get what I want. You see, I am on the same ladder that you want to get up on. I have done things that I was ashamed of when I did them, but I blocked it out to get what I want. I believe and believed in working hard to get what I want, but I, too, thought that it was going slower than I liked. I got some extra help. Now look at me. I have a wife and a family that is proud of me, and I am proud to have made sacrifices to get all that they needed. They don't have to know the details about it. They just receive and reap the rewards.

He looked me in the eye. "I am not ashamed to be the man that I am now. I told you no sex is involved. These are simple transactions that feed people's fantasies. It is not illegal to indulge others' fantasies and receive rewards for playing a few games. This is just like any business. You are fulfilling a need, and so are they. This is not forever. Before you know it, it will be over, and you will have what you want. This is your chance. What are you going to do?"

I looked at him and shook my head. I was so disappointed in myself.

"I'm game." Hearing myself say that out loud was bizarre. I thought back to when I went to the first party and saw crazy things. Now look at me. A willing worm on a hook. Bait. I was doing every *never* and *ever* I said I would not do. Control truly was an illusion.

"All you must do is a couple more sessions and you are free. You can get your promotion and be left alone."

"I have to say that I still don't like this, and I hope that you keep your word."

"I am a man of my word." He winked at me.

All the appeal that he had had in the beginning had melted away. I was a victim of my own lust and desires.

"How long have you been married?" I asked.

He looked at me for a few seconds, like he didn't want to answer my question.

"Twelve years," he finally replied.

"That's a long time to be married."

"True." He nodded his head.

"When did you start doing the wild stuff? Before or after your marriage?" I felt like all bets were off since we were in this entanglement. Why not ask what I wanted.

"Wow. That's a bold question." He looked uncomfortable for the first time since I had started being around him. "It started before, but I was not as active back then as I am now."

"You don't feel like you are betraying your family?" I asked.

"I am providing for my family." He looked at me like I was crossing a line by asking him about his family life.

"And eating your 'cake' too," I said and let out a light chuckle. I was feeling better from making him feel uncomfortable.

He laughed and said, "I see you are loosening up. I'll take credit for that."

"You would," I said with intentional sarcasm.

"Keith, you remind me of myself."

I looked at him out of curiosity. "How so?"

"You are strong willed."

"True," I agreed. I had thought he was going to say something sexual. Like I was a freak or something.

Our conversation continued until our food arrived, and then we ate in silence.

Chapter 42

Justin

I didn't have the evidence to say anything to Marlon about what I had heard. My gut knew better, though. I just didn't want to deal with this right now. I wanted to cut my heart out of my chest and throw it away.

These were the chances that you took when dating and falling for someone over a short period of time. I was just brokenhearted. I knew that I would have to deal with this at some point.

I stripped down to my bare body and jumped in the shower. I showered and cried at the same time. I felt like I was in Deborah Cox's song "Nobody's Supposed to Be Here." At some point, I lowered myself to the shower floor and let the water and the tears flow.

I left the shower after the water turned cold. I looked in the mirror at my puffy and red eyes. There was no way I was going to go out of the house today. It was a Saturday, and I was going to treat it as a complete day off from the world.

I mustered up some strength to lotion up my body and put on some silky pajamas. Silk against my skin always made me feel good. I fixed myself something to eat, and I poured a glass of wine to go with it.

After I finished eating, I grabbed my favorite throw blanket and curled up on the sofa. I planned on surfing the Net and distracting myself from the whole world. I sent my friends a text to let them know that my phone would be off and that I would be off the grid for a while.

It had been only a few days since I had found out about Marlon's family. Thinking about this sober was a monumental task. Every time I thought about Marlon and his family, I wanted to get a drink.

A wife and a kid. A wife and a kid. I repeated this in my head as I lay across the bed. I hadn't even gone to work today, because I didn't want to see anyone. I was hurting.

How could he do this to me? How could *I* do this to me?

I took out my phone and scrolled through the pictures of him and me together, and tears came down my face. Then I opened my text messages and looked at all the texts that we had shared. Some made me smile. Others made me laugh. Some made me angry.

I shook my head as more tears flowed. This broken heart was painful.

Marlon had been texting me over these past few days. I would answer by saying that I had a heavy workload this week and would be too busy to hang out.

I didn't want to give him a clue that I knew that he had a wife and a child. I was sure of it now. He was trying to play me, and I didn't like it. While only a few weeks had passed since I'd met him, I had fallen hard for him. I was mad at myself for trusting again. I had told myself I would not trust anyone very easily, but the heart wanted what the heart wanted.

Still, I wanted to get some more solid proof that he was the Marlon who had a daughter named Lisa and a wife named Angela. I knew that I had said I was sure that it was true. I just wanted to be 100 percent sure. I was currently at 90 percent.

I needed to get more proof; I didn't want to give up that easily.

I showered and got dressed. I was getting ready to see if I could get this evidence. The only way I could get it, I had decided, was to go to one of the sources.

I cautiously drove over to Judy's house, hoping I could somehow get in touch with Angela. I wanted to take her out to give her some relief and to be a friend. I knew that it was crazy to even think about doing something like this, but I didn't care. I needed to know about Marlon so I could move on without doubts pressing down on me.

I pulled up to Judy's house and parked my car. I sat in my seat for a few minutes, because I was nervous. I had to put on some serious acting to get what I needed.

I exited my car and walked up the steps to Judy's door. I took a deep breath and then knocked. It took a few minutes, but Judy finally made it to the door.

"Who is it?" she yelled through the door.

"It's Justin," I answered.

The door instantly swung open, and her smile greeted me.

"To what do I owe this pleasure?" she asked as she backed up and let me in.

"I wanted to check up on you. I was a little worried," I lied as I walked past her.

"Aw, you are such a sweetie," she said as she closed the door.

She was using her cane to get around and was moving better than when I had first come by to help her out. The therapy she was getting during the week was working. It felt good to see someone progress in therapy and life.

"Judy, you sure are getting that hip together. Soon you will be out there twerking and dropping it like it's hot," I joked.

"Boy, I think them days are over. All I want to do is drop it on this bed or the sofa." She laughed and then sat down.

"Judy, I'm not giving up on you. I might just have to give you lessons later down the road."

"We will see." She smiled.

"Did you need anything?" I asked.

"Well, I could use a fried egg sandwich. I was just about to get up and get to shaking some pans in there."

"I got you," I said and then walked into the kitchen. She had a few dishes in the sink, which I washed before I fixed what she had requested.

Once I had finished fixing her food, I served it to her.

"Justin, you are such a godsend. The person they sent to help me out before was trash compared to you." She took a bite of her food and then said, "And you can fry up an egg too. You can cook?"

"I do okay," I answered.

"This is quite tasty. It's much better than you think. Don't knock the talent that you have. Be the best egg fryer you can be," she said and then laughed.

"Thanks, Judy. I appreciate the love."

I watched her finish her food and then took the dirty plate back into the kitchen to clean it.

I was stalling, hoping that she would bring up her niece, but it wasn't happening fast enough.

I walked back into the living room. "Judy, how is your niece doing? I have been thinking about her ever since I left the other day."

"She is doing better," she answered.

"Does she have any friends?" I asked.

"Not really. She has been isolating herself since her marriage issues began."

"Well, I was feeling like I needed to help her out. She probably needs to get out. I was curious to see if you would deliver an invitation to her to get out. I know I don't know her, but I thought it would help her state of mind. We all need to get away from our troubles."

"Justin, that is so sweet. You are such a sweet guy."

"I do what I can." I gave her a broad smile.

"Let me call her and see if she would be willing to hang out," Judy said.

I watched as Judy pulled her phone out and dialed Angela's number. She quickly handed me her phone.

"Hey Auntie," Angela said when she answered the call.

"Hey, Angela. It's Justin," I said.

"Is my aunt, okay?" she asked.

"Yes, she is great," I replied.

"Oh, okay." She sounded relieved.

"I asked her to call you so I could see if you wanted to hang out. I know that you don't know me, but I wanted to treat you to a night out. We both need it," I said, and I let out a light laugh. I hoped she was up to it.

"Justin, that is so sweet. I am glad that you asked. I was feeling like I needed a night out too."

"Great. I will get your number from Judy so that we can coordinate details."

"Okay. I look forward to that," she said.

I handed the phone back to Judy and listened to them talk for a minute and then hang up.

I left Judy's, excited and nervous at the same time. I could be sealing the fate of my current relationship.

Life was not easy.

Chapter 43

Marcus

"How did I get to this place?" was the question I had asked myself many times over the past few days. I knew how. I was weak. I acted weak. I had to remind myself that I was not a punk. I had great wisdom and intelligence. My life had started out a bit rough, but I had never used that as an excuse not to push toward my dreams.

The past few weeks I had just wanted to give up and leave it all behind. All I had thought about was emptying my bank account and booking a flight to somewhere and not looking back. Atlanta was looking more and more appealing every day. All I had to do was swing by a Lowe's or a Home Depot and pick me up a few movers, and I'd be out of here in a few days. Yes, I had it all planned out. I wouldn't even let my friends know what was going on. I didn't want to have to make up any lies about why I was moving and all that stuff.

I knew that they would miss me, and I would miss them. While they didn't know what I was going through, I knew that they would not judge me. I was ashamed of myself. In the past I had chastised them about their choices without batting an eye. Now I was on the other side of the fence, looking at my bad decisions.

I also wanted to confess my deeds to my adoptive parents, but the look of disappointment on their faces would be too much to bear. They had instilled in me many values that I chose to ignore even now. "Come clean," was what I was taught. "Be honest with yourself and get some help. No one is alone in this world if they seek out the help they need."

I had a plan, though. I was going to become a player too. That was how you beat someone at their game. I was not going to be Michelle Obama. He went low, so I would go low.

Ronald wanted to play with both sides of the coin, and I was all for it. I was going to take a big chance and gamble.

I had made dinner arrangements at McCormick & Schmick's down at the Inner Harbor. Ronald liked to be treated like royalty. He thought that his manhood was a game changer. Admittedly, he was skilled in that area. But I was skilled in my own area.

I sat outside the restaurant, on the benches near the water, as I waited for Ronald to arrive. The atmosphere was very calming. The splashing sound of the water beating against the cement soothed my tension. The sun was beginning to set as several boats floated around the piers.

There was a light breeze that was rather cool, and I realized that I should have worn a light jacket. The breeze caused me to shiver, so I rubbed my arms to help warm up some. It didn't help, and I laughed at my foolishness.

"You are looking very tasty right now," Ronald said from behind me. I jumped a bit, because I was focused on my plan and the atmosphere of the Inner Harbor.

I turned and looked at the fine man who stood there with a smug look on his face. A chocolate drop with dimples was what he looked like.

It was a shame that he was so good-looking and had chosen to use people to get what he wanted.

"Did you miss me?" he asked. He had on a nice outfit that fit him in all the right places. It was a chocolate two-piece linen pantsuit that hugged his physique. He'd finished off the outfit with a pair of casual brown loafers. His hair was shaped up, and he had a very neat goatee. He was fine. I almost blamed God for this mess I was in. How could he make a man who was so good-looking and so devious at the same time?

"Actually, I did," I said with a smile.

"You caught me off guard with the 'We need to talk' text," he confessed.

"I didn't mean to," I lied.

"So why did you bring me down to this fancy restaurant?" he asked.

"Well, let's go inside and get something to eat. And we can talk."

"Cool," he said.

I headed toward the entrance to the restaurant, and he followed close behind me. We stepped inside and were greeted by the host. He was an older black gentleman whose smile was inviting.

"Good evening. Table for two?" he said.

"Please," I said.

"Follow me," he said and then led us through the restaurant.

The place was busy; waiters were attending to lots of occupied tables. The music was classical, and it put me at ease. This restaurant was known for its great seafood and fancy décor. Chandeliers hung from the ceiling; small accent candles and flowers decorated the tables. This was nothing like Applebee's or TGI Fridays.

"Where did you bring me? What kind of fancy place is this?" Ronald quizzed as he looked around the place and then at me after we were seated.

Ronald wasn't completely ghetto. He looked like he belonged here, because he was well groomed and knew how to put on an act. I was impressed.

"I thought that you were treating me so nice that I would return the favor," I replied.

"Ronald can do that to you." He spoke in the third person and then laughed. "A little dab will do ya." He laughed again.

He was too much. It was sickening, but I had to keep going.

"You are absolutely correct," I confessed.

I went on. "You know, this was supposed to be just a 'hit it and quit it' type of deal for us. But things changed when you thought that it would be more beneficial for you to blackmail me. I was hurt by that," I said as I looked him in the eyes.

"So, you trying to make a brother feel guilty for giving you what you wanted?" he said.

"I wanted a body part, not a hostage situation," I said.

"I told you before that I was an opportunist. You knew my record before you approached me. You act like you're the victim. You got what you wanted, but it was more than you bargained for," he said. He spoke the truth.

"You are right," I agreed.

"You can't say that I didn't hold up my end of the bargain. You just thought that I was a freebie. I've learned that everything has a cost. You never estimated what I would cost you."

I had to admit that he was not lying. I played the game and lost. Or so he thought.

"Ronald, you wore me down. That is why we are here," I confessed.

"I'm confused," he said.

"It has taken me a minute to confess this. I am shocked by it myself . . ." I looked him in the eyes. "I'm in love with you. I want us to be exclusive."

"What?" He had a shocked look on his face.

"I said that I am in love with you," I repeated and then smiled.

"I think that is a personal problem," he said and then laughed.

"I'm serious. I want you to cut Melissa off and move in with me. I want to take care of you."

"I'm not committed to anyone but myself," he announced.

"I am giving up my license to practice in Maryland and looking for a new line of work so that we can be together," I continued.

I reached into my front shirt pocket and pulled out the fake resignation letter I had written on my computer. It was on official letterhead and all. I slid it over to him and watched as he opened it.

"I'll give you some time to break it off with Melissa. I have plenty of money saved, so we will be financially secure for quite some time."

"This is not real." He looked at me with an expression of doubt on his face.

"This isn't a game, Ronald. I don't play with my feelings. When I have a man, I go hard for him. You can ask any one of my friends. I love hard."

"I'm not for no gay relationship. You are just a wet hole and free money." He looked angry now.

"Well, I am claiming you, and you have no choice," I stated.

"*Claiming* me? Nobody owns me," he muttered. "Plus, I don't believe a thing that you said or this fake resignation. I'm calling your bluff."

"This is no bluff. I am giving you some time to break it off with Melissa, or I will."

"You are not built like that," he said. He was sure of himself.

"You are not the only one that has proof of our relationship. In fact, I have more than you do. One anonymous picture of us together sent to Melissa, and it will be over. You will be mine for sure."

"That's not going to happen," he responded heatedly.

"Ronald, today one picture or video can ruin a man's whole life, even a regular man like yourself. One post across social media would devalue you in no time. Nobody would want you anymore. You would be damaged goods. You don't even have to be on any of the sites to be a victim. The word would get back to you in no time."

"You're lying. You don't have anything. I'm still calling your bluff."

"I'm not lying. I love you and want you. I will do anything to keep you. I love hard." I stared in his eyes. "Let's enjoy our first date of many. Let's not start this off the wrong way," I said.

"If you think that I am going to sit here and pretend to be on a date with you, you must be crazy," he snarled.

I picked up my phone and pressed SEND on the mini video I had of us in bed during one of our hotel excursions. My face was blotted out to protect my identity, but Ronald was shown clearly.

He picked up his phone and looked at what I had sent him. I watched as his eyes got bigger.

"That is the short version. I have video from a few of our past encounters. They were supposed to be for my pleasure later, but now I must use them for other things."

He didn't have anything to say. It was the first time I had seen him speechless.

"Don't worry. As I said, I will give you time to break it off with Melissa. Also, I would order a big steak for dinner if I were you. I plan on working you out later tonight."

I was hoping that my tactics would scare him off and that he would decide to leave me alone.

Minutes later, the waiter delivered our entrées. The food looked exquisite as he sat each plate in front of us. The culinary presentation by itself was worth the money. Despite the circumstances, I would be enjoying my steak, potatoes, and vegetables.

"This looks good," I said as I glanced down at my plate.

"It's cool," Ronald mumbled.

I cut into my steak, took a bite, and a soft moan of pleasure escaped my mouth.

Ronald just looked at me as he cut his own steak and chewed on it.

"Taste good?" I asked. I was having fun.

I felt like I had the upper hand, so why not have fun with it?

Ronald didn't have much to say the rest of the night. What could he say? I had turned the tables on him. It felt good.

Chapter 44

Evan

Paranoia was my frame of mind right now. I was doing the unthinkable for me. I had had Allen on the brain from the moment I woke up this morning. It wasn't because I loved him. It was because today was the day that I had an "appointment" with his father.

I couldn't believe that I had sunk this far. Being under the influence of lust was just as bad as addiction to alcohol. When your flesh was constantly calling the shots and you gave in to desires foolishly, your life could quickly become one big mess.

I had been dealing with this problem for quite some time. When I was a young teen, being gay was really challenging for me. This was not to say I had it harder than other kids because of my sexual orientation. But it just didn't help. My emotions and urges were raging right around the time I moved into the group home. I was glad I had the friends that I had there, because having people around you who knew what you were going through helped quite a bit.

Back then there were boys all around me every day. Some knew how to handle homosexuality, and some did not. Some straight boys were insensitive and immature about the subject. But what could I expect? We were all rejected boys with little life experience. We all had our own stories to live out.

Anyway, there was one incident I was involved in at the group home that kept me together for a few years.

One day I was on kitchen duty with Mr. Wilson. It was just us two, and we were having fun. I had had a crush on him since I first met him. He was a very attractive guy. I tried to spend as much time with him as I could. He laughed and joked with me, and I confused that with affection. From time to time, I would watch him walk around the house. I would admire his behind, and it would make my manhood rise.

Just as we wrapped up drying the dishes, Mr. Wilson turned to me and said, "Thank you, Evan, for all the help around the house today. I really appreciate it."

"No problem." I smiled.

"Now, give me a hug so that you can get ready for bed," he requested with outstretched arms after he had put the last dishes away. This was a normal display of affection that he and his wife shared with us. They were always openly affectionate toward us.

I leaned in to receive his hug. It was tight, and it made me feel good. Before I pulled away, I lowered my hand and squeezed his behind, causing him to push me away.

The look on his face was one of pure anger. "Sit down." He pulled out a chair for me to sit down in. He then pulled out of a chair for himself and sat down.

For a few seconds he just sat there and looked at me. Then his face softened. "That was completely inappropriate. That action could get you put out of here if I tell my wife."

The thought of being moved to a new place with new people scared me to death. I didn't want to start over again. "I don't want to leave here. I'm sorry. I won't do it again," I cried softly.

"Look, this is between us, but I will tell you now that you get one pass with me," he said with firmness and authority.

I nodded my head.

"Evan, I know that you are young, and you don't fully understand your emotions. Sometimes as boys, we tend to act and not think when we have urges. It can be confusing. You just can't go around putting your hands on people without their permission. It is very dangerous to do that. And when you add in the same sex, that could cost you your life or freedom. Not everyone is as understanding as me. You understand?"

"Yes, sir." I nodded.

"From now on, keep your hands to yourself. I would hate to lose you to some violence because of a mistake. So do me a favor and try to control yourself. Sex can lead to some very sticky situations, and you don't want to end up somewhere or with someone because you didn't know how to control yourself."

"I'm sorry, Mr. Wilson. I won't do it again."

"I accept your apology. Just keep your hands to yourself by yourself." He laughed because he knew that I knew what he meant.

Minutes later I walked up to my room a changed guy. While I was still attracted to him, I never again made the mistake of trying anything with him or with anyone else in the house.

I kept my hands to myself, like he had suggested.

Now here I was, years later, tangled up in a web of deception. My attraction to an older man was fueled by thoughts about Mr. Wilson. I knew all of this was wrong, but I had a monkey on my back, as they said.

I had decided to rent out a private room in a gym far from the place where I normally held my sessions. I could not afford for Allen to pop up while I was at work, and even though I had told him that I was going to be busy, I didn't trust him to stay away.

I didn't know what to expect from Allen's father. He would text me pictures of his body. The parts only his wife should be privy to. He was a great-looking guy and moderately in shape. He could use my services for sure, but I knew that he didn't want to be whipped into shape in that way.

He wanted special treatment, and I would be offering it today.

At home I had packed a bag with all my protection in it for this occasion. I wasn't completely careless. I cared about my health. I didn't do STDs.

Allen's father arrived at the gym on time and was dressed in exercise attire: a tank top and some spandex shorts. He filled out his shorts nicely for an older man. I would say he was in his early fifties, and he had tight curls and gray hair close to his temples.

I made sure I locked the door behind him. What I was doing could get me banned from most of the gyms and possibly locked up.

"Wassup, Evan?" he asked once I had turned my attention to him.

I was thrown off by the language that he had used. He came across as trained and educated. Ebonics coming from him was strange, even though I had encountered him only twice before.

"Hey, sir," I answered.

"Call me Eddie." It was the first time that I had heard his name. He didn't seem like an Eddie, if that made sense.

"Okay . . . Eddie," I said.

"You are looking good." He looked at me with lust in his eyes.

He walked up to me and then circled me slowly. I had on a tank top and some regular gym shorts. He rubbed his hands up and down one of my bare arms and then squeezed my biceps.

"You are in good shape too." He leaned in close to me. "And you smell good. That's how Daddy likes it."

Hearing him call himself Daddy was a turn-on, and it caused my manhood to grow.

"Is Daddy going to get a good workout today?" he asked as he moved his hand under my shirt and massaged my pecs.

I closed my eyes and enjoyed the pleasure that he was giving me. Oddly, it reminded me of Allen. He was just as attentive and detailed. "Like father, like son" had a whole new meaning for me right now.

"As long as our deal is still in play," I told him.

"You don't have to worry about my son. I have him covered," he assured me.

I was hoping that he wasn't lying to me to get me to do his bidding.

"I'm a full-service kind of guy," I assured him. I felt a pang of guilt because the smiling face of his wife popped into my mind. Eddie massaging my manhood snapped me out of my guilt. I was pretty sure that I wasn't the first guy he'd been with, and I probably wouldn't be the last.

He palmed his head and lowered himself down to his knees. He didn't hesitate to mash his face into my lap and pleasure me through my shorts. My manhood grew harder as he continued. Next, he pulled down my shorts and worked my manhood with his hands.

"You are a big boy, aren't you?" he said as he worshiped me with his mouth.

He didn't have any problems making it disappear into his mouth.

I enjoyed every moment of it. Any guilt I was feeling didn't have a chance. This guy was a professional. He had his son beat by a long shot.

"Take your time," I urged him, because he was going to town.

"I can't help but enjoy this. It's been a minute for me. I want to enjoy this," he replied and then continued to work me over.

I just closed my eyes and let him enjoy himself. Who was I to hold him back?

A few minutes later he got up and began to pull down his pants. He lowered himself until he was on all fours.

"I'm ready for the full service," he announced. He looked back at me as he wagged his tail like a dog.

I went over to my bag and pulled out the necessary protection and then primed myself to go all the way. I turned on some exercise music to help cover up any sounds that we would make.

"Smack it," he ordered.

I did as he asked, which caused him to wag his behind some more.

I kneeled behind him and did what he'd come here for.

I entered him, and he instantly became animated with pleasure. He pushed back onto me and rode me like a jockey. He was truly a professional at this.

I flipped him into all types of positions, and he took every one of them like the champ he was. He was giving me a workout too. I couldn't deny that he was making me work hard.

We finished up, and he exited the room. I made my way to the shower room and cleaned myself up.

Chapter 45

Keith

I was back at it again. I was at the house with the bunch of fantasizers. I walked into the house like I had other times I'd been here. I was scared this time too. I didn't know what to expect. This place had all types of weird things going on in it.

Costumes, role playing, and even animals were all fair game in this place. I could see why they made you sign a nondisclosure agreement. However, they didn't have to worry about me spilling any of the things that went on in here. I wanted to forget about this stuff as soon as I left this place.

Who in their right mind would want to brag about anything they did or saw in this place? The shame I felt here was astonishing. And it was mainly for me. I knew that I had let myself and my parents down. I know that my friends would look at me differently if they ever found out about this.

I had to admit that I was a prude when it came to sexual stuff in public. I was not into public displays of affection. I liked to be a quiet indoor freak. That was probably why I didn't have a man now.

Anyway, I was greeted by the person who normally took me to my fantasy room. As we stood there, I saw a few young white boys who were dressed as different animals and were being walked around on leashes. I was glad that I was merely a watcher, or an observer, as they called it. There were all types of titles in this place. I was amazed at all the underworld stuff that was going on here. It was more than met the eye for sure. I couldn't even look at people the same anymore.

I was led to a room and told to go in, just like before. I opened the door and was greeted by a cold room and silence. I shivered a bit as I stepped inside the room. The lighting was low, and this gave me a gloomy feeling.

Again, there was a lone chair and a table sitting in the middle of the room. Long black curtains blocked off what looked like half of the room. I walked over to the chair and sat down as curiosity enveloped me. Then music started to play. But this wasn't any type of happy music. It was organ music, and the sound reminded me of death. It made me feel like death was in the room. I didn't play when it came to death and funerals.

Suddenly, the black curtains slowly began to open. I couldn't believe my eyes. A black casket lay in the middle of the floor. It was closed. I couldn't believe that a dead body might be lying in front of me.

Everything in me was telling me to run out of the room. But I couldn't move. It felt like I was stuck. And then I had a sudden urge to see if there was a dead body in the casket. I had almost gone into mortuary science in college but had decided against it at the last minute. Dead bodies didn't bother me. It was live people who made me nervous.

A man came out of one of the doors inside this room. He wore an all-black dress, and a veil covered his face. He even had on black high heels. He walked slowly as he sobbed into a black hand-kerchief. They really took this role-playing stuff seriously.

He kept sobbing as he leaned over the casket, like someone would do if they were being overly dramatic at a close loved one's funeral. He began to rub and shake the casket, and then he fell to the floor, as if he had passed out. He came to moments later and stood back up. He rubbed the casket again, and then he opened it.

I leaned forward in anticipation. I watched this guy get in the casket and started grinding and sliding all over the body. Then he proceeded to pump the chest, like he was performing CPR.

There was some wild stuff going on here. I was flabbergasted.

Then he climbed back out of the casket and motioned toward it with his finger, as if to say, "Come here."

Suddenly, the body in the casket sat up. I gasped.

It was Kingston. I looked at him as he climbed out of the casket in nothing but Speedo briefs. I was instantly turned on. He was a fine man and built like a god. Chiseled muscles all over.

The guy in the dress stripped down to his underwear and high heels. Kingston proceeded to push the casket out of the way to reveal a small bed behind it.

They both climbed on the bed and began to wrestle seductively. Both were naked before it was all over. They pleasured themselves, then exited the room. I wasn't pleased this time. Death mixed with sex was an absolute no-go. I was ready to get out of there. And that was what I did.

Chapter 46

Justin

I pulled up to the restaurant that I had invited Angela to. It was on the outskirts of Baltimore County. A nice little Italian restaurant that I came to from time to time when I wanted a good pasta dish. It was quiet and not too fancy. I generally enjoyed good service and food here.

I parked in the parking lot next to the restaurant. I let my car run as I waited for her to arrive. A couple of good songs came on the radio as I waited. I scrolled through some social media sites and laughed at the silliness that was portrayed on them. I was trying to distract myself from being where I was right now. I was ready to say, "Forget it," and go back home.

It was too late, because she pulled up and got out of her car. I got out of my car and waved in her direction. She saw me and came right over.

"Hey, Angela. I'm so glad that you could make it," I said.

"I am too." She looked a little hesitant. I would be, too, knowing that we were practically strangers.

"Let's get us some good food and relieve some stress," I suggested. "They have some good drinks in here, too, if that's your thing."

"I love me a good strong drink." She let out a laugh as we both made our way into the restaurant.

We were quickly seated. The waiter came and took our drink orders.

"Justin, it is so nice of you to do this for me," Angela said after the waiter walked away from our table. "I was hesitant to come because I don't know you. Aunt Judy convinced me to come so that I could get a break. She said that you are a good, caring person. She said that you listen well and offer some good advice."

It felt good to hear good things said about me. But it also saddened me a bit because my motives weren't truly pure.

"Judy can be quite persuasive, can't she?" I smiled.

"My auntie has been one of my biggest supporters currently in my life. Ever since my mother passed away, she has been right there." I could tell she was getting emotional.

"Everyone needs someone they can count on," I said. Thoughts of Marlon filled my head, and I felt myself getting emotional too. I didn't plan on that.

The waiter came back with our drinks and then took our appetizer order.

When he left, I went on. "You are so right. I am going through something with someone too. That is why I invited you out to eat. So that we both could get away from our problems temporarily."

"I know that is right," she agreed.

"I don't know why people can't just be up front with someone they say they love," I said.

"How long have you been dating this person?" she asked.

"It's been about two months," I answered. "I think that is long enough for someone to give me the truth about important parts of their life. Is that too much to ask for?"

"I think that's long enough. What were they hiding?" she asked me.

"The truth about a past relationship. Well, I think it is over. I am not sure. I don't know how to approach them about the subject."

"Don't ask me about that, because I am still working through my soon-to-be ex-husband's betrayal," she said after she took a sip of her drink.

"You didn't have a clue, did you?" I asked.

"Marlon and I had been high school sweethearts off and on again. I heard a rumor or two about him in our senior year, but he convinced me that it was someone hating on him and trying to get my attention."

"Oh, wow. That is crazy." I shook my head.

"I never investigated, because he had never lied to me before. Plus, Marlon was talented, and there were people that were jealous of him. He was good-looking, and most of the ladies wanted him." She briefly smiled, like she was going back over some good memories in her head.

"Do you think he might change his mind and come back?" I asked.

"I don't know. Every time I look at my daughter, I hope and pray that our family can be reconnected. The problem is he will not talk about anything but our baby girl when he calls me."

"Relationships can be so iffy," I said.

"It is making me sick just thinking about him leaving me for a man. It makes me feel like less than a woman," she admitted.

"From what I see, it's his loss."

"Thanks." She smiled. "That means a lot to me."

"I meant it. You are a stunning woman with a great personality." I meant what I said. I could not lie about that. The situation made me nervous, though, because it seemed like Marlon could change his mind and go back to her.

I wasn't trying to push her toward him or away from him. I just wanted to know if their marriage was truly over. I knew that what I was doing here was bold and that I was clearly crossing the line. I wasn't even sure what I wanted now. This was a family, and clearly, she wasn't over him.

Now I was conflicted.

"Have you been on any dates?" I asked.

"No. I don't have it in me," she confessed.

"Has anyone shown interest in you?" I asked.

"Truth is, I would not have noticed. I've been in a fog most of the time. Besides, I just need some time to get Marlon out of my system."

"True. Rebound love is the worst," I mused. I was hoping that I wasn't in a rebound situation myself.

"Plus, my baby girl is going to need some time to adjust," she added.

"True. That is a heavy one for a child stuck in the middle of a breakup."

I felt bad because I wanted to keep dating Marlon, but I didn't want to be the one who hindered a reconciliation. And what kind of person would I be if I had this information and continued to date Marlon?

Technically, I didn't have this information. Neither party knew that I knew. I was a victim of circumstances here. I was hurting too. I loved Marlon. He had said he loved me.

The waiter came back with our appetizer order. I'd ordered one of my favorite dishes, but my emotions were running too high for me to really enjoy it.

"Justin, I am so glad that you invited me out. Our conversation has given me some stuff to think about. I just didn't know if I should fight for my family or let it go. I don't want to be a quitter, but I don't want to be a stalker either."

"Life is all about choices, and we all must make them. Good, bad, or ugly."

We continued to talk about life and other things as we ate our food.

An hour later, we got up from the table.

"I needed this," she said as she pushed her chair in. I could see tears welling up in her eyes.

She walked around the table and pulled me in for a hug. It was a tight hug. You would have thought that we were long-lost friends. It made me emotional. I held my emotions in, though.

We left the restaurant, then parted ways, and as soon as I got in my car, I burst into tears. It was a "sob and snot" type of cry. You would have thought that someone had died. I felt guilt. And I felt shame. I realized that I had been acting out of character. I thought, Was this all worth it? I cried all the way home.

I couldn't bear to be alone, so I freshened up and made my way to the club.

Chapter 47

Marcus

Today I was glad to be working. I had a full day of clients, and their problems were a great distraction for me. Anybody's problems seemed better than my own. I was a therapist who needed therapy.

After my last client left, I decided to treat myself to dinner. Food was a part of my therapy. I cleaned up my office and gathered my things, intent on heading over to Famous Dave's. It was a barbecue rib spot that I lived for.

I exited my office, and as soon as I closed the door, I was greeted by Melissa and Ronald, who were lurking in the hallway.

To say I was surprised was an understatement.

"Hey, Doc," Melissa greeted me with a smile on her face.

I tried to hide my surprise, but I was stunned. "To what do I owe this pleasure?" I asked as I looked at her and then at Ronald. He had a wide smile on his face. He was truly a pain in the butt. He was like a flea on a hound dog.

They were holding hands like they were lovers.

"We wanted to take you out to dinner for all the hard work you do in my life," Melissa answered.

"Oh, really?" My eyebrows rose in curiosity.

"Well, it was Ronald's idea. He said he couldn't believe the turnaround in my life from the sessions that I have had with you."

"That is so nice of him." I smiled in his direction. "I'm sorry, but I have plans. I must give you a rain check."

"Oh no, Doc. We would really like to treat you. It would break our hearts if we couldn't," Ronald said. He was so slick and sexy. I hated it.

"Yes, Doc. Please make room for us. We would really like to treat you," Melissa begged.

"I don't think that would be appropriate," I said as I looked at her and then Ronald.

"Aw, you can break the rules just this one time," Ronald said with a sly smile. I wanted to punch him right in the face.

"Give me a minute, so I can see if I can break this date." I walked away from them and pulled out my phone and pretended that I was calling someone. I was glad that I had not turned on my phone's ringer, since I wouldn't be caught in a lie with an incoming call.

I was away from them, so they couldn't tell if I was talking to someone or not. I made hand gestures for them so that they would think it was a hard task to get out of my date.

I walked back over to them with a smile. Even though I was not happy at all.

"I can come," I said.

"Great. We are going to have a good time." Ronald grinned.

"You can follow our car," Melissa said and then they turned and walked down the hallway.

I slowly walked behind them as Ronald squeezed and played with her behind in front of me. I knew that he was playing with me after the meeting we had had the other day. I guessed he was calling my bluff.

We rode the elevator down to the lobby. Ronald continued to shower fake affection on Melissa.

"Baby, you smell so good," he said as he kissed her neck.

She giggled. "Stop, baby. You are making the doctor uncomfortable."

"Doc knows what true love looks like. He is good with this show of love. Right, Doc?"

I nodded my head. I was hoping to get this over with as early as possible.

Once outside, I got in my car and waited for them to pull off in their car. I followed them for about a half hour before we reached the restaurant they had chosen. It was an Italian restaurant called Mario's Italiano. I'd been here once before, and the service had been cool. As I recalled, it was a mid-level restaurant. It was a three on a scale of one to five. The décor was red-and-white-checkered tablecloths over wooden tables. I remembered that the place had smelled heavily of Italian seasoning.

I pulled into a parking spot and looked around. The parking lot was half-filled, which meant we wouldn't have to wait for a table. I contemplated just pulling off and saying that I had an emergency to attend to. But I didn't. I just didn't have the strength to lie this time around. I was doing too much of that as it was. I signed up for more torture.

I exited my car and met them at the restaurant's entrance.

"Ohhh, Ronald this is so fancy." Melissa hugged and squeezed him.

"Nothing but the best for the best. Right, Doc?" Ronald said.

"Sure is." I smiled as displeasure filled my heart.

"Let's go in and enjoy ourselves," Ronald declared.

We walked into the restaurant and were greeted by a hostess. I noticed that the restaurant was filled mainly with couples. Black couples, gay couples, old and young couples. It made me feel odd and out of place.

We were seated in the middle of the establishment. Instrumental music was playing in the background, and candlelight filled the room. This would be a perfect date if it wasn't for me being a third wheel.

"Doc, thank you for coming," Melissa said.

"No problem," I answered.

"Doc, I can't tell you how much the work you do in Melissa's life has changed my own. You are a miracle worker. We owe you more than just dinner. We owe you big."

"I love what I do. I care about people getting better and living better."

The words that I had just spoken were sincere. Unfortunately, I was doing the opposite. I was pooping where I ate, and that was a big no-no.

"He takes real good care of me so that I can take care of me and my man." She reached over and kissed Ronald on the lips.

The waiter came over to our table and took our drink orders. I ordered some wine, because there was no way that I was sitting through this charade without a liquid aid to help me through it. The waiter left and soon came back with fresh bread and butter. Melissa dove into the basket and gobbled up a piece of bread.

"Baby, looks like you are hungry," Ronald observed as he picked up a piece of bread and then spread some butter on it. He looked at me and smiled.

"Ronnie, you know what I like," she said with a giggle.

Ronald looked at me as he began to feed her the piece of bread he'd buttered, and then he put his mouth on the other end of the bread. He worked his way through it until he got to her lips, and then they kissed. It made me sick. These *Lady and the Tramp* wannabes.

I picked up a piece of bread and buttered it. I always enjoyed great bread when I went out to eat. I was going to enjoy something about this night. Even if it was just the bread.

They continued to be playful with each other, and I tried to block them out. I looked at the menu, and then I scrolled through my phone, pretending that it interested me more than they did. The more I tried to ignore them, the more Ronald played it up.

"Doc, are you okay?" Ronald asked. "You don't look too good."

"I feel great. It's nice to see people in love. With so much scamming and cheating in the world, it's just nice to see a stable couple," I lied. I hoped he felt all the sarcasm that laced my answer.

"We owe it to you, Doc," Melissa said.

Shortly after, the waiter delivered our drinks and took our dinner order. I made sure that I ordered a nice big steak and a baked potato with the works. I wanted at least to be full of food and not just regret tonight.

"I need to use the bathroom," Melissa said before she pulled away from the table. She got up and then disappeared.

"So, you thought that you could just threaten me and I was going to roll over!" Ronald barked as he leaned over the table.

"I still have my cards. You need to just back off. I got less to lose than you do."

"How do you know that I am going to lose?" he snarled.

"Look at you. You are all flash and no substance. You are dead on the inside," I countered.

"You think that you are the smartest one at this table, but you are not."

"We will see," I shot back.

"Bet," Ronald seethed.

Melissa came back after a few minutes of Ronald and me just staring at one another across the table.

"I feel so much better," she said as she sat down in her seat. "Did you miss me, baby?" She leaned over and gave Ronald a kiss.

"Baby, I sure did," he said as he got up out of his chair. "But I know not to miss you anymore."

I watched Ronald go into his pocket and pull out a small black box. And then he lowered himself to one knee in front of Melissa.

"I know that I have treated you badly in the past, but today I want to vow to cherish you forever and ever. Would you do me the honor of becoming my wife?"

My mouth hung open from shock.

"Yes, baby, yes!" Melissa leaped up out of her chair and hugged Ronald tightly around his neck, and then she jumped up and down. Tears ran down her face.

I wanted to cry, too, because it seemed like he had the upper hand now. Now that he had proposed to her, he was going to have more control over her. He was probably going to convince her to continue seeing me so that he could continue to blackmail me.

I sat there and watched them kiss, and the people in the restaurant cheered them on.

The only way out of this now was for me to hand in an actual resignation letter to the board of health. I was sick to my stomach.

Chapter 48

Evan

I was really feeling some type of way after sexing Allen's father the other day. And not in a bad way. I mean, the man knew how to get down with it. They said experience was the best teacher, and Eddie had taught me that he was the experience that I had been missing out on. It almost made me forget all about Allen.

It was a Saturday morning, and I was in my home and lying across the bed, hoping that Eddie had convinced Allen that it was foolish to want me. He had said he would take care of this matter, but I had my doubts. How could I trust someone who was cheating on his wife with his son's boyfriend?

I was startled by a knock on my front door. I got up and made my way to the door. I looked through the peephole and then opened the door.

It was Allen. He had red eyes. I hoped that it was from marijuana and not from crying. He was such an emotional person.

"Baby, I need you," he said as he walked toward me and then wrapped his arms around me and pulled me into a tight hug.

I closed the door behind him, and we stood by the door and hugged. Since I was a nice person, I made an effort to squeeze him back.

"What happened?" I asked and then pulled away. I looked him in the eyes and admired his handsome face. He had some of his father's features, which I could see now, and it turned me on.

"We need to talk. Can we go in the living room?"

I nodded my head yes and then led the way. Curiosity caused my mind to wander as I sat down on the sofa. He sat down on the sofa, too, but he was a cushion away from me.

"What happened?" I asked.

He ignored my question. "Do you love me?" he asked.

"I like you a lot, Allen." I purposely avoided saying that I loved him. *Love* was a strong word, and I just wasn't there. I didn't want to break his heart. And I also didn't want to give up the attention he had been giving me. He knew how to kill a brother with kindness. He was spoiling me, and I loved it.

"I know that you do. Someone is putting doubts in my head, and I hate it."

"Wow. That's not good." I told him, not knowing what to say. It seemed to me that what I'd said was appropriate.

"It wasn't good to hear either. Especially coming from my father." Tears started to roll down his face.

"What did he say?" I asked.

"I don't even want to repeat it," he responded.

I sat there in silence for a moment. I was concerned about what his father may have said about me.

"It was that bad, huh?" I finally said.

He really looked like he was emotionally spent. His father must have been harsh with him.

"I need something to drink," he said, and then he got up and went into my kitchen.

He came back five minutes later with two glasses of water. He handed me one, and he sat down and began to drink the other.

I waited patiently for him to finish his story.

"I really thought that my father liked you," he said as he sat his glass on my coffee table.

"I thought that he did too," I agreed.

"Well, now he's on some crazy stuff. Talking bad about you." He shook his head.

"What did he say?" I asked.

"I don't even want to repeat it," he told me. Because I know it's not true." He scooted closer to me. He paused for a beat. "Would you ever cheat on me?" he asked me.

"If I had feelings for someone else, I would be honest enough to tell you. I think you deserve that much respect. I hope that you would do the same." I said that as I looked him in the eyes.

I was such a hypocrite. I hated myself right now. I didn't even recognize myself.

"Baby, I would never cheat on you. You mean the world to me. You are my future husband."

"I appreciate your attentiveness toward me. It's nice," I said.

"I'm not finished. There's another part," Allen continued.

"What else did he say?" I asked.

"He said that you came on to him," he revealed.

"He did?" I acted surprised.

"I know he was lying from the jump," Allen said.

"Why would he say that I came on to him? That is crazy." I tried to look shocked and hurt. I wanted to lay it on thick.

"I know. He said that I must stop seeing you, because you are going to do nothing but hurt me, like all the other guys I've dated."

"Oh, wow," I said. "What are you going to do?"

"He is threatening to put me out, since I am working on my second college degree, and he is paying for all of it. My parents said that I didn't have to work if I was in school, bettering myself. Now he is using it against me." He huffed, and then the tears started to fall again. "I might just end it all if I have to give you up."

I didn't look at him when he said that last part. He couldn't be that attached to me. That was not good at all.

"That is crazy." I shook my head.

"I know. That is why I am here. I was thinking that I could stay with you, since we are about to get married." He gazed at me, and I saw that his eyes were still glassy. As I looked at him, all I could think about was that he was suicidal.

I had to think quickly, because there was no way that I was letting him move in with me. And he was talking about suicide . . . This was out of hand.

"I don't think that is going to happen. I think that I can talk your father out of it. He looks like a reasonable man. He's just acting out of emotion. Give me some time before we make any moves that we might regret."

"My father is stubborn, Evan. I don't know what you could possibly say to him that would make him change his mind." He looked at me like he didn't have any hope.

"Do you trust me?" I asked.

"Yes, I do," he said as he nodded his head.

"Good," I replied.

"Baby, can I pay you back for coming to my rescue one more time?" he asked.

"You sure can." I smiled.

Allen eased even closer to me and began to kiss me on the mouth. I knew that I shouldn't, but I let him continue.

His hands found their way to my lap, and he began to massage my manhood.

If there was picture of *messy* in the dictionary, it would be one of me.

I let Allen finish me off, and then he went into the kitchen and fixed my breakfast. He was waiting on me hand and foot, like he normally did.

I was out of control.

Totally out of control.

Chapter 49

Keith

I sat in my office chair, which was turned toward the window. I looked out at the bright sunny sky. People were walking around outside, going about their day, lost in their own world.

Everyone had their own little world inside the larger world. We planned only for ourselves. We let people in to serve a purpose, and once they did, we dismissed them. It was called using people.

I was so mistaken to think that Kingston had my best interests at heart. He was out for himself, and I couldn't blame him. Still, it felt like having a broken heart but not being in a relationship. And I felt stupid and ashamed.

These visits to the fantasy house were too much for me. I wondered how Kingston put up with this stuff and how he had got started. He had really put on a performance the other day with the casket and all of that. I could not get those memories out of my head. It was like I couldn't unsee what had happened.

I closed my eyes at night, and the crazy images just wouldn't stop appearing in my mind's eye.

All of this for a promotion. Who does that?

Well, it was apparent that many people did things that I would deem strange in order to get ahead in life.

I wanted to get out of this mess. But I had no idea how I was going to manage that.

There was a knock on my door just then. I knew it was Jennifer. I didn't want to talk to anyone today, but since I had a job to do, I had to interact with people.

"Come in," I called out.

Jennifer walked into my office. Her bubbly personality was on full display.

I had the sudden realization that needed her presence right now. My funky thoughts were getting the best of me.

"Keith, I have a problem," she said as she sat down in the chair in front of my desk.

"You do?" I asked.

"Yes. It's this person that I am working with. It seems he has been giving me all kinds of shade lately," she said with sass.

"Who is it?" I asked out of curiosity. I needed to hear about somebody else's problems right now. I wasn't big on gossip, but today I was going to indulge.

"I ain't one to gossip, but it is you." She pointed to me.

"What?" I looked shocked. "How have I been shady toward you?" I asked.

"You have been ignoring my texts and calls. You didn't even say hi to me this morning when I passed you in the hallway." She rolled her neck a bit.

"Jen, It's not personal. I'm sorry. I just been going through some stuff," I said, apologizing.

"You know that I am used to your funky mood swings, but not giving me a little bit of attention broke my heart."

"Jen, I am going to make time for you outside of work in a few days. We can hang out as soon as I handle some personal stuff."

"Boo, I was all kinds of worried. I was getting ready to make a house call." She burst out laughing.

"I didn't totally ignore you, though. We talked at work," I offered.

"That was some *dry* communication. It looked like you were on autopilot or something."

"I was, and I still am kind of. I just got to work through some stuff."

"Keith, get it together, so we can get together," she said, and then she got up out of her chair. She exited the office and closed the door behind her.

She had made me smile.

I turned my attention to some emails. I had tried to focus at work these past few days, but my choices were getting the best of me, and my mind kept straying.

I went through some of my social media profiles just to lurk and see who else was going through what. I knew that I wasn't the only one making crazy choices. I browsed for about a half hour. Then I turned my chair and looked out the window again, watching people scurry about, their lives consuming them. It was a familiar scene.

As my mind drifted, there was another knock on my door.

"Come in," I called out again as I swung my chair around to face my desk.

This time it was Kingston. He came in and took a seat across from me.

I just looked at him. I didn't have anything nice to say to him.

I wanted to go back to the beginning and ignore his advances and his charming personality. It seemed like those were nothing more than lures to pull me close and then get me involved in this sick game. I had fallen for it, but I now saw the real him. He was still handsome, but he was much less appealing.

"You're not happy to see me?" he asked.

"No," I answered. I focused my attention on the computer screen instead of him. I was madder at myself than him.

"You didn't enjoy the show I was in?" he asked. He smiled like he had given an Oscar-winning performance. But it was porn combined with a twisted fantasy and delusion.

"It was different," I said, speaking plainly.

"Aw, you are hurting my feelings."

"Well—" I stopped short of going on a rant.

"I can see that you are not in the mood."

"I'm frustrated," I said.

"With?" Kingston asked.

"How long are you going to drag this thing out?" I asked.

"You are not enjoying your adventures?"

"I want what was promised to me." I looked at him in his eyes.

He smiled at me. I wanted to smack the smile off his face.

"I'm not enough? It's what you wanted originally," he said.

"Excuse me?" I looked at him like he was crazy.

"Your eyes were all over me when I first walked in the door. You didn't think I noticed how you sized me up?"

"I size up everyone I meet who is new," I responded.

"Do you watch the crotches of ladies too?" he asked. He had a smug look on his face.

I threw a question back at him. "Did you enjoy being watched?"

He laughed. "I enjoy watching you enjoy me," he said.

"Kingston, I will admit that I was attracted to you in the beginning. I made the mistake of not wanting to get to know you as a person. I wanted to sex you. I admit that. I will also admit that my attraction for you has all but gone away."

He got up from the chair and unzipped his pants and let them fall to the floor. He pulled out his manhood and began to wave it.

"I know what you saw the other day is still on your mind. You know that I still have you wanting this." He moved around the desk and then stepped close to me. I instantly recoiled. I was not putting myself in another bad position, no matter how tempting it was.

"I think that you need to put that away. This is not professional. I've changed my mind. I don't want a promotion if I must do crazy stuff to get it."

He backed up several steps. "I'm sorry. I'm sorry," he said as he put himself away. Then he walked back around the desk and sat back down in the chair.

We just sat there in silence. I didn't have much to say.

"What are we going to do about this?" I asked, breaking the silence after a few minutes had passed. "I want the promotion that I was promised."

"I have to talk to my friends and see," Kingston replied.

"What do you have to *see*?" I asked. "I fulfilled my end of the agreement." I was boiling mad that I had to keep jumping through these never-ending hoops to get what I was promised.

"You are just going to have to be patient. I don't run the show."

"I'm losing my patience with all of this," I snapped. "So I'm about to expose all of this. I don't care anymore."

"I don't think you want to do that," he said and then stood up. "These aren't the types of people you want to get upset."

"I don't care anymore. I traded in my dignity and pride for a promotion, and the goalposts keep getting pushed back. How long am I supposed to put up with this? I am a man. I can only take but so much."

Almost ready to cry, I looked at him, but I held back my emotions in an effort to retain the little bit of dignity I had left.

"Don't do anything that you might regret," he cautioned as he walked toward my door.

"It's too late for that," I said. I spoke from the heart. I didn't know if I had the heart to do anything, but I had to put the threat out there that I would not take this lying down.

What was the worst that he could do to me?

Chapter 50

Justin

I had the red carpet laid out. I was supremely dressed. I had cooked a fabulous meal. And my house smelled fantastic. I had some Anita Baker playing on my surround sound.

My heart was fluttering in my chest.

Marlon was coming over.

My emotions were all over the place. I had spent most of my day crying and listening to sad love songs.

There was a buildup of pain on the inside, and I just didn't want to live sometimes. I didn't know how this night was going to go, but I had to press through this no matter what happened.

The doorbell to my apartment rang, and I walked to the door to answer it. I opened the door to Marlon, who was looking so handsome and well groomed.

"Hey, sir," I greeted him.

He came in, and I shut the door.

He reached in for a hug. He pulled me close to him and squeezed me tightly.

"You smell so good, baby," he moaned. His hands moved up and down my body.

"I know," I replied. "You do as well."

"I missed you," he said as he pulled back and looked me in the eyes.

I tried to hold his gaze, but I couldn't manage this for very long. I looked away because I didn't want to lose him, and looking at him made my heart melt again. I didn't want to lose the nerve to ask him about his past.

"I missed you too," I told him, and then I turned and walked toward the living room.

"And I thought that you were trying to get rid of me." He laughed and then swatted me on the butt.

It felt good when he did that. I missed his attentiveness. He made me feel wanted.

"You are the best thing that has happened to me in a long time," I said as I sat down on my sofa. He settled next to me.

"I can appreciate that. I feel the same way." He leaned in and kissed me on the lips. It was a long kiss. I had to pull back to get some air.

"Ooh, Marlon. Them lips of yours," I moaned.

"You don't know how hot you are making me." He reached his hand over and gently rubbed the side of my face. His hands were so soft.

"Calm down, sir. I have a whole evening planned."
I got up and went into my kitchen and brought
back a tray of fruit and cheese.

I sat the tray down on the coffee table and then
went back into the kitchen to get the wine and the
glasses that I had chilling.

"Oh, you are going all out. This is how a man
likes to be treated. I could get used to this." Marlon
grinned as he looked up at me.

With the music playing lightly in the background, everything seemed perfect.

I still didn't have the slightest idea how I was
going to bring up his wife and daughter. I didn't
think it was a good idea to be direct. I had seen
the loving and caring side of him quite often. I had
never seen him angry.

I had to calculate my moves correctly to get the
information that I wanted.

"I can get used to giving this to you. All of it." I
stood the wine bottle and the two chilled wine-
glasses on the coffee table, then sat down. After I
poured wine into both glasses, I handed him one,
then lifted the other.

"To our future," he said as we held our glasses up
and clinked them together. Then we drank from
the glasses before setting them down.

Before long, we both finished our wine. I filled
our glasses again, and then we took turns feeding
each other fruit and cheese. I turned the music up

when one of my favorite songs came on: "Chanté's Got a Man," by Chanté.

Marlon got up off the sofa and then pulled me up. He drew me close to him, and we started slowly dancing to Chanté's beautiful voice. I closed my eyes and laid my head on his shoulder. I was in heaven.

When the song ended, we sat back down on the sofa.

"Let me go check on dinner," I said. I got back up and walked toward the kitchen.

I had a rotisserie chicken with veggies cooking in the oven, and it smelled just as good as Marlon did.

"Marlon, go sit at the dining room table. I am about to bring the food out," I called out to him.

I fixed both of our plates and then brought them into the dining room.

"I am so impressed with you," he said, complimenting me.

"No problem," I said as I sat his plate in front of him. Then I sat down with my plate.

The scent of the candles on the table lifted my mood quite a bit. But thoughts about what I was going to say to him still swam in my head. I tried to block them out and let nature take its course.

"I hope that you like it," I told him.

We both lowered our heads, and he prayed for the food. Then he took a forkful of chicken and placed it in his mouth. I watched him closely, awaiting his reaction.

"You can burn in the kitchen too," he said moments later. "I am a blessed man."

"That you are." I smiled.

We both ate our food and then rested in between bites as we sat at the table. I ate until I was full. He seemed full too.

"Let's go back into the living room so that we can talk," I said before I grabbed our empty plates and put them in the kitchen.

After a slight cleanup, I went back into the living room and plopped down next to him on the sofa.

"Baby, can we talk?" I asked.

"Uh-oh," he said as he looked at me and then laughed. "Is my life on the line?"

"It's no biggie. I just wanted to get to know you better and vice versa. I think that it is important in the beginning of a relationship."

"Absolutely," he said as he nodded his head.

"All right. Me first." I fidgeted in my seat for a second before I asked him the first question.

"What's your favorite color?" I asked.

"Green," he answered. "What's yours?"

"Brown," I answered. "What is one of your biggest pet peeves?"

"Dishes in the sink, I guess," he answered. "Yours?"

"Same as yours," I answered.

"Birds of a feather." We said it in unison and then burst into laughter.

"Would you ever go back to your last relationship?" I asked when our laughter had died down.

"Oh, you not playing games, are you?" he said and then chuckled. "I don't leave relationships unless it is all the way over. No need to go back to pain and heartache," he said with a somber expression on his face. "What about you?" he asked.

"I feel the same way about it as you do. No going back," I answered.

He nodded his head. "What do you like about me the most?" he asked.

"I like the way you smile. Especially them soft lips." I leaned in to kiss him again. His soft lips made me very horny.

"What do you like about me the most?" I asked when the kiss ended.

"Your giving personality. You know how to make a person feel good and how to keep them happy. I need that. The club life can be stressful and unpredictable." He leaned over and kissed me again.

His answer to my question calmed me down and made me feel like I could trust him. I decided I didn't have to worry about him leaving me for her. I was convinced we would figure out the rest in time.

I just had to wait for him to share what he wanted to share about his past. Going through the transition from being with a woman to being with a man—and having a child and a marriage in the mix—probably was stressful, and I didn't want to make things worse for him by throwing in my concerns.

Chapter 51

Marcus

I guessed I would be a third wheel for life. Ronald proposing to Melissa right there in from of me in the restaurant had just blown my mind. *How can I top that*? I asked myself.

It was like I was trying to win a football game. It all had to do with who had the ball last and could score with almost no time left on the clock. It seemed to me that I had the ball right now, but I was on fourth down, with only inches to go.

But it might as well be fifty yards.

I was alone in my office. I looked around at the pictures and degrees on the walls. I was still proud of myself. But I had to shake off this doom and gloom I was feeling. I was a man. I had to step up.

I had made these choices in my life, and I had to be a man and handle them. I had already made up my mind that if I lost my job, then that would be it. I would have to change professions. I was a smart guy. I could start over. I could do something else.

The only problem was figuring out what that would be. What other skills did I have other than making bad choices? I loved helping people.

What it all boiled down to was that I didn't want to give up my livelihood.

I now knew that no one could mess up your life more than you. I wanted to foist some blame on someone else, but I could not find anyone who had put a gun to my head.

I was arrogant in thinking that I was smarter than most people and that I could fix my problems with the same mind that had caused them. It was insanity to think so.

I had done the unthinkable. I had invited Ronald out for what would hopefully be one last romp. I wanted to offer him one last intimate moment—and a large sum of money.

I would dangle five figures in front of him to get him to leave me alone. That was most of my savings, but it was a last-ditch effort. I was desperate.

I gathered my things and made my way to my car. I got behind the wheel and drove. I prayed the whole way there. I knew it was now too late to involve God in my plans. But I still did it anyway.

I pulled into the parking lot of a motel that was one of the ones we used to play around as kids. It was on the outskirts of Baltimore, near a highway, with scattered trees in the back. It was a place where you went when you were trying to be discreet.

I paid the person at the front desk and went up to the room. It wasn't a crappy room. There were plain tan curtains in the window, a matching carpet that had no stains, and the bed had been made up with burgundy linen of a fairly good quality. Whenever I booked a room, I was doing a dirty thing, and I didn't want to do it in a dirty room. I had some class about my trash.

I prepared the room to my liking and waited for Ronald to arrive. I put on some light jazz with the Bluetooth speaker that I had brought from home and had connected to the music on my phone. I sprayed the bed down with cologne. These hotel rooms had a dimmer light switch, so I dimmed the lights and lit a candle.

The knock on the door let me know that Ronald was on the other side of it.

I walked to the door and opened it. His smile greeted me, along with some good-smelling cologne. He knew how to market himself and be presentable.

"I knew that you would give in," was the first thing that he said to me as he walked past me with a confident stride. I wanted to clip him just to see him hit the floor and wipe that smile off his face. I needed some pleasure other than sex right now.

"Yes, you are the winner," I said as I closed the door.

"We are both winners. You got me, and I got me. A win-win." He laughed.

"I don't know what I would do without you," I said, with sarcasm dripping from every word.

"You know, Marcus. You are a very good opponent. I underestimated you," he admitted.

"That's nice to hear," I responded. His compliment really did make me feel good. I was surprised.

"Well, let's get this party started. You been holding out on me, and I want a re-up on that good stuff you got. Melissa has been holding out on me, too, for some reason. My hand has never been my main source of satisfaction. It has always come out the runner-up." He laughed. He began to undress. At one point, he dug in a pants pocket and then threw a gold condom on the bed.

"Wait . . . Before we start, I need to ask you something," I said.

"I hope you are not going to try that love thing you did the other day. I don't have time for it. I already proposed to Melissa . . . begrudgingly. I don't want to do any more. It's draining."

"I just want to make you an offer, so that you'll leave me alone."

"What kind of offer?" he asked. His interest was piqued.

"I have ten thousand dollars to give you if you leave me alone and convince Melissa to stop seeing me as well," I proposed.

"I'll think about it," he said. "Now, come over here and get on those knees of yours. I need some extra attention tonight." He smiled at me.

A moment later there was a knock on the door, and we both froze.

"Ronald, I know that you are in there," Melissa called from the other side of the door.

My heart started beating fast, and I looked at Ronald.

"I'm not going anywhere, so just open up the door!" she commanded.

He slowly walked to the door. He opened it, but only a peep. "Why are you following me?" he muttered.

"Because I rented a car for you to go wedding planning, and this is what you are doing. You are in some uppity motel with some trick! I knew all this good behavior was an act. Nobody like you changes just like that. I was just giving you some room to hang yourself."

"You didn't trust me?" he asked her. I wanted to bust him in the head myself for asking that crazy question.

"Let me in!" she ordered, because he had his foot on the bottom of the door to prevent her from pushing it.

"No," he said matter-of-factly.

Then Melissa stuck a gun in the gap of the door. Ronald eased back, with his hands up, and

Melissa charged over the threshold. She kept the gun aimed at Ronald as her eyes darted over to the corner of the room where I had taken refuge.

"Doc, what are you doing here?" she asked, with a surprised look on her face. She closed the door behind her.

"I . . . I . . ." I tried to talk, but the words wouldn't come.

"He was giving me some therapy. We wanted to surprise you," Ronald explained hastily.

"Then why are your clothes unbuttoned?" she shot back.

"I just came out of the bathroom," he answered.

"You zipper is down. Why?" She waved the gun around a bit. It caused me to jump.

"I forgot to zip it."

"How convenient. I don't believe it." She had anger all over her face. She was clearly unstable at this moment.

"Doc, what were y'all really doing?" She looked at me and then back at him.

"We were . . ." I paused and looked at Ronald. He seemed to have good answers, so I decided to let him roll with it.

He didn't say anything. He just looked at her and then back at me.

She looked around the room, and then, suddenly, her gaze froze. Her eyes had zeroed in on the condom on the bed.

"Y'all were getting it in?" She looked at me and then at him.

I was speechless.

"It's not what you think," Ronald pleaded.

"Ronald, I am not stupid. I know math. One plus one equals screwing. Now, both of you, get up against that wall. I must decide who betrayed me the most."

"Melissa, think about this. It's not worth it. Don't do this," I pleaded as Ronald and I stepped over to the far wall and leaned against it.

She aimed the gun at both of us and then shifted back and forth between us.

She fired the gun.

Chapter 52

Evan

These two guys were two sides of a single coin. One of them was soft and attentive, and the other one was rough and submissive. I had both sides of the coin, but I couldn't keep going on like this. I had to get these two guys out of my life for good. I just couldn't do it anymore. They were both crazy and obsessive.

My good looks and bad decisions had got me into a lot of trouble. And it hadn't helped that I loved sex.

I had to meet up with Eddie and try to convince him to back off Allen a bit. I could not and would not let Allen move in with me. I didn't want to live with anyone yet. I didn't like to share my space. More importantly, Allen was too clingy. I could take this behavior in small doses, and so we saw each other only from time to time. Living together would lead to one of us getting hurt.

I decided to meet up with Eddie at Edwardo's, the very restaurant where Allen had introduced me to his parents.

I drove my car, and he drove his. When I pulled up to the restaurant, I simply sat in my car. I didn't want to get out. I didn't want to confront this situation, but I had to do it. I finally got out of my car and walked toward the restaurant's front door and went in.

"How are you, sir? How can I help you?" the hostess greeted. She gave me the once-over, which let me know that she wanted more, but she wasn't my type, and I was already in a terrible entanglement. I didn't want any more trouble.

"Yes, I need a table," I said.

"Follow me this way." She walked in front of me and led me to a table in a corner.

I sat down and looked around. This was a romantic restaurant. There were nice decorations here. Fancy tablecloths, lit candles, smiling people enjoying their food. Classical music was playing. But none of that mattered, since I just wanted to talk.

I sat there for a few minutes, just enjoying the atmosphere. The people around me were engaged in conversations with each other. There was laughter and chitchat. There were even a few people eating alone, letting their phone be their date.

Eddie showed up a few minutes after I did. He walked over to the table and sat down. He smiled as he looked across the table at me. I just stared at him. I had to be about my business. I didn't want to continue living life sneaking around.

I got right down to business. "Your son said you threatened to kick him out if he continues to see me. You said that I was a cheater."

"Technically, you are a cheater," he said, reminding me of the obvious.

"I know that. Why couldn't you just tell him something else? Now he wants to move out of your house and into mine. I can't do that. I like my solitude."

"What should I have told him?" he asked.

"Anything but that," I muttered. "Now I have to find a way to convince him to stay with you."

"You are a smart guy. I know that you can do it," he smirked.

"You are trying to get me to do your dirty work?" I asked.

He wasn't a dummy. He knew what he was doing. He wanted more leverage so that he could get more sessions.

"I think I could get my wife to lure him back in. She is very fond of him and can work him better than I ever could, but that is going to cost you." He laughed.

I didn't like that laugh. It sounded evil.

"Eddie, I'm not playing these games. It was a huge mistake to even deal with you. You are trying to work the middle. So I am just going to have to let him move in with me and deal with it."

"You are a tough young man. I admired that."

"I do what I can. I was raised in the hood. Don't let the good looks and nice clothes fool you," I told him.

"Can we eat?" he asked.

"Sure. I am a little bit hungry."

We placed our order, then sat and ate and talked about nothing in particular. I was just trying to get out of here and head to the club. I needed to get out and hang out with my boys tonight.

We parted ways as soon as we walked outside the restaurant. The daylight was gone; the nighttime had arrived. I planned on drinking plenty of alcohol tonight. Nothing could stop me from getting to it.

I walked to my car, and before I could get in it, someone came up behind me and pinned me to the driver's door. I felt something hard—a gun?—being pressed against my back, so I didn't move.

"So, you think you can just play with someone's heart?" the person snarled. I recognized the voice, but I could not believe this was happening. I tried to turn and see if it was who I thought it was, but the attacker had on a balaclava.

I didn't dare answer the question.

"You are going to pay for playing with me. I am going to Taser you, and then this knife is going to finish the job." The attacker waved the knife in my face by reaching around me from behind.

My heart was racing; I was panicking, since I saw no way out of this situation. I hadn't been oblivious to the consequences of my actions of late, but I hadn't thought that it would go this far.

"Please, don't do this! I'm sorry. I didn't mean it. I'm sorry. I'm so sorry," I pleaded.

"Round one . . . ," I heard my attacker say, and the sound of a Taser being turned on let me know they were not playing. I felt the hot current as soon as it hit my body. I slid to the ground and jerked as I hit the pavement. The last thing I remembered was someone hovering over me.

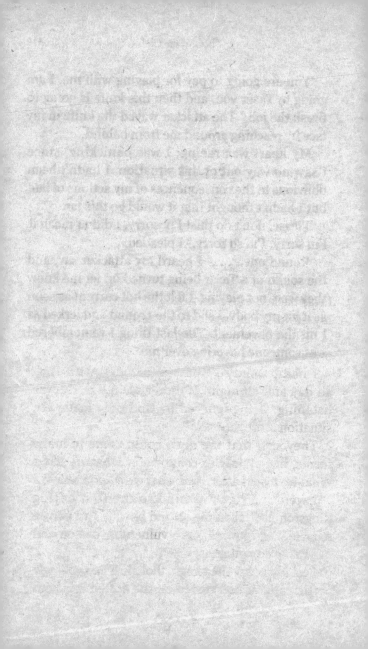

Chapter 53

Keith

I sat in my office, just looking around the room. I was backed into a corner. A corner that I had put myself in. I was over this whole thing. I was tired of feeling sorry for myself. I just wanted to get out of this mess.

I had prayed to God and pleaded with Him all day and all night. It didn't seem like He was listening. Being ignored by God only made the situation more dire.

They said that the devil could come in many forms, but mainly in the form of what we liked. What we lusted after. And what we couldn't have.

I went back in my mind to the first outing Kingston had taken me on and how he had played me. He had known I was a vulnerable person and had taken advantage of me.

I couldn't play the victim, though. I had willingly participated. I had signed on the dotted line with the devil and had lost. I had played myself. I had screwed myself, and not in a good way.

As these thoughts were swirling through my mind, there was a knock on my office door.

"Come in," I called.

"Hey, boo," Jennifer said as she entered my office.

I was beginning to love her presence more and more. She didn't know it, but she was a light for me at work. She was a godsend. I played off my appreciation for her well by appearing nonchalant, but I really enjoyed her presence.

"How is your day going?" I asked her before she could ask me.

"First, I'm a little astounded that you asked me first," she said, and then she smiled.

"I am reevaluating my life and how I treat people. Starting with you," I said candidly.

"What has you on this serious trip? I mean, you are serious about most things, but today I actually hear some care in your voice."

"Changes in life do that to you," I told her.

"Keith, what's wrong? You're not sick, are you?" she asked as she leaned across the desk. She had concern written all over her face.

"Jen, I am not sick. I am frustrated," I confessed.

"What are you frustrated about?" she asked.

"Have you ever made some choices that caused you some deep regret?" I asked her. I looked deep into her eyes so that she would know that I was serious about this talk.

"Yes, I have, but I got over it. We all make bad choices." She paused for a moment. "You act like you killed someone," she added.

"No, I didn't kill anyone. I want to kill *myself*. I'm in some deep stuff," I revealed.

"You are not serious, are you?" she asked, her brows knitting.

I looked at her before I answered. "I'm close to it. I mean, I know what other people feel when they off themselves. I have never had these thoughts before on a serious level."

"You have to go see somebody about this. Don't you have a friend who is a therapist?"

"Yes, but I'm too ashamed to talk to him about it. Also, I can't talk about it, because I signed some paperwork that says I can't talk about it," I informed her.

"What kind of stuff were you doing that had you signing a nondisclosure agreement?"

"I wish I could tell you, but I'm too ashamed to tell you as well," I said and then looked down at my desk.

"That is crazy. Can you tell me who it involves?"

"I can't tell you, but if you guess, that would be okay."

"Is it someone that works here?" she asked.

I nodded my head.

"Is it a man or a woman?" she asked.

"Man," I answered.

"It's Kingston," she said.

I didn't respond.

"Oh my God." She covered her mouth with her hand to muffle an emotional outburst. But her voice was loud, nonetheless.

"Be quiet," I ordered. We were at work during business hours, and so was Kingston.

"I'm sorry, but I can't believe it." She stared at me. "Are you and him sleeping together?" she asked.

"No, we are not," I revealed.

"Why can't you talk about this stuff if you are not having sex?" she asked.

"I just can't."

"Kingston must have a secret. A big one," she mused aloud.

"Everyone has secrets," I told her.

"Not one that you must sign paperwork to be quiet about. That's a deep secret. I want to know."

"No, you don't," I told her.

"You are right. I don't want to know. I *need* to know." She thought for a moment. "Keith, I make all kinds of subtle advances toward him. Some are not so subtle, but he always gives me the brush-off. I am a beautiful chick. He doesn't even look. I say to myself all the time that he must be dedicated to his job, his wife, or he's a secret boy chaser."

"You are something else." I looked at her in amazement.

"No, I'm observant. He is in your office more than he's in most of the others, so I'm going to say that he likes the boys. You don't even have to say anything, because I feel it in my gut. My gut doesn't lie."

I shrugged. "I don't know what you are saying. This is your imagination running away from you, if you ask me."

Just then, there was a knock on the door.

"Come in," I called.

Kingston stepped into my office. I looked at Jennifer, hinting with my eyes that she should keep her mouth closed. She could be quite blunt at times.

"Hey, Kingston," she said as she looked him up and down.

"Jennifer," he said in a dry tone. He really didn't even look at her.

"That's all I get?" she said.

He looked at her and then replied, "I'm not in the mood."

"I bet," she snapped at him.

"What?" he snapped as he looked at her. I had never seen him this way before. He looked angry.

"I didn't say anything," she said, feigning innocence.

"I need you to leave. We need some privacy," he told her, and then he looked at me.

"Oh, of course you do," she said as she got up out of the chair.

"What is that supposed to mean?" he growled. He looked like he was going to hurt her.

"You spend a lot of time in here with him. The office is talking. But you didn't hear that from me." She gave a sarcastic laugh.

"You!" he yelled as his head swung in my direction, and then he lunged across my desk and knocked me off my chair to the floor. Everything on my desk came crashing down on top of us. We both got tangled up in computer cords, and paperwork was scattered everywhere.

The expression of rage on his face, I was sure, stemmed from a sense of betrayal. I struggled to contain him, but his hands made their way around my neck in no time. I threw punches that landed, but they didn't deter him one bit. I was trapped. I gasped for air as he tightened his grip on my neck. I could see Jennifer trying unsuccessfully to get him off me, and then I began to lose consciousness.

Chapter 54

Justin

I was smiling again, despite the fact that I still had some reservations about Marlon and his undisclosed family situation. I was keeping a close eye on the situation, but I believed him when he said he wouldn't go back to any of his exes.

I was so glad that I didn't act a fool when he came over to my apartment for dinner that evening and go in blazing with accusations. That would not have been a good look for me. I would have looked like a child with no training.

I was proud of my maturity. It took so much to mature and care about others and their feelings. It had never dawned on me that Marlon may have been struggling with being a bisexual. He may have been wrestling with that his whole life.

When you were dating and you threw in a child and a soon-to-be ex-wife, that was a recipe for confusion. I didn't want to be a part of any confusion if I didn't have to be.

In the back of my mind, I worried about meeting Angela again.

When the truth got out, how would I explain these meetings to either of them?

When I got home from work, I headed straight to the shower. I was going out to dinner with Marlon tonight. I was super hyped. I felt light as air.

Once I had dried off, I sprayed myself down with a body oil called Extreme. I loved the way it made me feel. Next, I put on one of my favorite outfits. It hugged my body but also let me breathe. The weather today was warm for Baltimore, so the lighter fabric was perfect.

When I exited my house, the sun was just beginning its descent. I got behind the wheel and headed to the restaurant that he had chosen for us. He was treating me tonight. As I drove through the city streets, I had on some R & B, and the latest hits were flowing through my speakers. Everything seemed right in the world. You couldn't tell me anything.

I drove about twenty-five minutes away from my home to a nice restaurant that appeared very romantic on the outside. I parked my car in a parking lot near the restaurant and walked about half a block to the entrance.

I could see Marlon standing outside, waiting for me. The sun was almost down now, but I could see the smile on his face and knew it was for me. I was in love.

He looked so handsome. He had on some nice slacks and a blazer, with a colored T-shirt underneath. I really wanted to give him a big wet kiss, but I didn't want to cause a scene. Some stuff people just couldn't handle.

"Hey, sir." I walked up to him and gave him a hug. I nice long hug too.

The restaurant had outside tables, and the night sky was so inviting that I wanted to dine alfresco. It went with my upbeat mood.

"You look ready to eat," he said to me and then laughed.

"Well, I did hold off on lunch today, because I knew that you were treating. I must take it where I can get it," I said and then laughed too.

"I see no problems with that," he replied, smiling. He held my gaze for a moment before he added, "Well, let's go in and get this party started."

I nodded, and he let me lead the way into the establishment.

We were immediately greeted by the hostess. "Would you like to eat inside or outside?" she asked us.

"Outside," I announced, chiming in before Marlon could say a word.

"Sure. Follow me," she said.

We followed her as she guided us to a table outside. The outside tables were on a gated-in patio surrounded by a small black wrought-iron fence. There were other couples dining outside, and small candles flickered lightly on their tables. It felt so romantic.

"I am so glad that you asked me out tonight. I needed it. Today was a hectic day with two of my patients." I told Marlon once we were both seated.

"I'm glad that I could be of service." He gave me a bright smile.

Our waiter soon came over and took our drink order. Marlon ordered water with lemon. I opted for a glass of wine.

It didn't take long for the waiter to come back with our drinks. We didn't waste any time ordering our food, and then we just chilled and talked.

"How was your day?" I asked him.

He paused for a moment, and then he began to talk. "It was interesting. You remember the other day, when you were talking about ex and stuff?"

"Yes," I said as I nodded my head. My heart started to beat faster, and my mind went all over the place. I was already in the worst-case scenario.

"Well, my ex has been pressuring me and being aggressive. It's just draining me."

"Well, this is your time to relax and let go. I'm sure the problem will take care of itself," I assured him.

And then the strangest thing happened.

Angela popped up out of nowhere, as if our conversation had conjured her up out of thin air. "So, this is who you left me and your daughter for?" she hissed.

Her sudden appearance caused me to jump.

"What are you doing here! Why are you following me?" Marlon uttered between clenched teeth as he stood up.

"I need to know why Justin didn't tell me that he was dating you." She looked at him and then at me, her eyes narrowed.

"You know her?" Marlon asked me, incredulous.

"Not really . . ." It was the truth. I really didn't *know* her. We had just met.

"He is a health-care provider for one of my aunts," she explained, her eyes hard. "He took me out to eat and pretended to care about my life, and now I find him with you," she went on. "Justin, I really liked you, and all this time you were playing games." She pointed a finger in my face.

"I really didn't mean to hurt you," I said with genuineness in my voice. "I'm so sorry."

"Angela, don't do this. This is not the time or the place. Can we do this another time?" Marlon asked with pleading eyes.

I looked around, because it was clear to me by the sudden hush on the patio that this was becoming a scene. I didn't like my life to play out in public like a reality television show.

"When?" she asked.

"Tomorrow. I'll come by tomorrow," he answered.

"Don't lie to me, Marlon," she said before she stormed off.

He sat back down and then looked at me. "We have a lot to talk about, don't we?" he said quietly.

"Yes, we do," I answered.

The waiter brought us our food just then, but we didn't get a chance to eat.

Suddenly, we heard tires screeching, and then we saw car headlights headed in our direction. We tried to run along with a few of the other patrons, but it was too late.

Chapter 55

Marcus

There was a quiet in the room that matched the urgency of the current circumstances. It was cold in this room, and there were machines beeping and tubes running in and out of holes in his body. None of us could have imagined this scene before us right now. One of our friends was knocking on death's door.

Fear and pain had taken away our speech, but the tears flowed freely. We looked at each other with unspoken hope and the blatant fear that was undoubtedly throbbing in our hearts and minds.

What could we have done to prevent this? was what I wondered.

We all were standing close to the door, threatening to run out. I wanted someone to pinch, punch, or slap me to awaken me from this nightmare. But no one moved. And I couldn't. I just stared at the sight before me. Selfishly, I was glad that it wasn't me who was lying there. I was not ready to die. But I knew that my friend in that bed felt the same way.

I was praying to God for a miracle. I was not a praying man, but I was hoping that God heard me loud and clear. It was His call, though. I was not naive in that area. I knew who oversaw it all.

It seemed like an eternity, but we had been there for only a few minutes. My body involuntarily started to tremble. Someone grabbed my hand to calm me down. The warmth of the palm of their hand eased my mind.

I was going to be the brave one. I willed myself to move. One step in front of the other, I walked toward that bed. My heart was thumping, and my mind racing, but I did it.

I reached out and placed my hand on his hand as it lay beside his body. It was warm. It gave me hope. I needed it. Soon the others followed. They did the same thing I had done, reached for his hand. We all held on to him, hoping that this wasn't the last that we felt his warmth.

Memories of us at the club flooded my mind. The laughs. The cries. The fights. The cursing each other out. The raunchy talks. I was gripping it all in my mind.

The fervor behind my prayers to God was akin to the intensity of the police beating on the door in the middle of the night. I wanted His full attention when it came to my friend right now. I needed Him to answer me. I needed my friend to make it. I willed it with all of me. I just needed Him to agree with me.

"Come on, God! Do it for me! I don't ask for much. Do you hear me, God!" I didn't realize that I was praying out loud until the others started embracing me and crying at the same time.

All we could do was wait.

And that was what we did.

We waited.

Justin lay in that hospital bed. A car had jumped the curb at a restaurant and had plowed right into him and his friend, along with two other people.

Justin had taken the brunt of the hit. His friend had been hurt badly as well. The other two people had been released from the hospital earlier today, after receiving care for minor injuries.

They said it was a random drunk driver who had lost control of his car. Justin and his friend had just been in the wrong place at the wrong time. The doctors had said that his chances of making a full recovery were strong, but that it would be a long one.

About twenty minutes later, we all left the hospital room and walked across the hall to the visitors' lounge to a get a breather. It was not easy to sit in that hospital room and look at our friend in that condition.

The first thing we did in that lounge was have another group hug. We squeezed each other long and hard. We cried some more, too, because we all felt so bad about Justin and we all had some serious stuff going on that could have ended our lives.

I knew that I was grateful to be alive.

"I can't imagine my life without any of y'all," Keith whispered as tears fell down his face.

"Me either, even though y'all get on my nerves at times," Evan said and then laughed.

It was great to find some laughter at a time like this.

"We have to take turns coming up here and visiting him," Keith said. "He made it his business to take care of others, and we will do the same for him."

We all nodded our heads in agreement.

Even at a tough time like this, it was always necessary to focus on the positive. These terrible incidents in our lives would teach us to communicate better and more frequently. It was the truth that we had dropped the ball on helping each other out. We had almost let our pride take us out.

We had to get back to our roots. We clubbed together, but we didn't communicate on a deep level with each other.

We were all going to need therapy after this. It was necessary.

Chapter 56

Evan's Epilogue

Healing was the order of the day for me. I had a hard time coming to terms with finding out that it was Allen's mother who had tried to take me out in the restaurant parking lot that night I had dinner with Eddie.

She would have succeeded, it appeared, if it hadn't been for an off-duty police officer who had just happened to be sitting in his vehicle in the parking lot after getting something to eat from an eatery nearby.

She got some time in prison for aggravated assault.

I lived with the thought that I had almost lost my life.

As my boys and I sat in that hospital room, watching Justin go on a roller coaster of surgeries and procedures, it made me appreciate life more. It made appreciate my friends more. We had taken life for granted until it was almost gone.

I made it a point to help Justin with his recovery, just so I could be a helping hand.

I had thought I was doing something meaningful by helping people get in shape and kick bad eating habits and so forth. Now I knew that life was so precious and that being fit was certainly good, but having all the pieces of one's life together like God had made it was better.

There were doctors out here doing their best to put people back together the best they knew how. Justin was a perfect example. I was learning to treat people the best I knew how, like they were a work of art.

Today I was meeting up with Allen and giving him a sincere apology. He was a good guy, and I had done him wrong.

I chose what I would call a classy joint as the place to meet up. At five o'clock, I arrived there, and when I stepped inside, jazz music was playing. I was led to a nice table, and before long I was swaying in my seat. As I looked around the restaurant, I saw that it was filled with people from all ethnic backgrounds. It felt good to be in a place where everyone was enjoying their lives and other people's too.

I watched as Allen made his way into the restaurant and walked over to the table. He looked good. I had always thought that he was good looking, but today he had an extra glow.

"Hey, Allen." I stood up and reached out to hug him. He was hesitant at first, but then he hugged me. I squeezed him tight. He felt good.

"Hey," he said as he pulled away.

"You look good. Did you lose some weight?" I asked.

"Yes, because I haven't been eating. I found out that my father was involved with my boyfriend, and I lost my appetite." He smiled. But I knew that it was a fake one. That was a shot at me, and I knew it. I took it, because I deserved it.

"Have a seat, so that we can talk," I said.

He did as I'd asked. He didn't look like he wanted to talk, though.

I retook my seat. "Allen, I invited you here to tell you how bad I feel about how everything went down between us," I said, with a look of sympathy.

"So, you are sorry for sleeping with my father, which caused my mother grief and agony and is costing her jail time."

"I'm sorry. I didn't mean for any of this to happen. I tried to tell you that I wanted to slow down, but you weren't listening."

"Now it's my fault that you couldn't control your manhood and commit to one person."

"I'm sorry I hurt you," I said, apologizing again.

"The sad thing is that I still love you, but every time I look at you, I imagine you doing my father." He looked heartbroken. And it was my fault. I was a creep and a jerk.

We sat there in silence for a few moments, trying to figure out what else to say. I couldn't muster up another word. He looked broken, and I couldn't fix it with an apology.

"Can you tell me that it was worth it? Was getting to bend my father over worth breaking up a family? My mother will never be the same. Never. She thought that she had the perfect family, and now it's shattered."

I spoke honestly. "Allen, I will take some of the blame, but I will not be the scapegoat for your family and their crazy secrets." I paused so he could absorb what I'd said. "You father told me that this was not his first time sleeping with men. It was bound to be exposed by someone. I was just in the right place at the wrong time."

"How convenient," he retorted.

I just looked at him. Tears welled up in my eyes. He was damaged goods now. He wasn't good for anyone.

"Have you thought about getting therapy for the pain that you are in?" I asked him.

"I'm too embarrassed to go. How can I go into a place and talk to someone I don't know about my Daddy issues?" He looked at me with shaky eyes. He was unstable.

"I don't know. I can admit to you that I wouldn't know how to talk about it to a stranger either."

"Why would you suggest it, then?" he asked.

"I just thought it might help you."

"I think that you are here just to relieve your guilty conscience." It looked like he wanted to spit in my face as he uttered those words.

"No, that is not what I am doing. I am truly sorry. I can't say it no other way," I told him honestly and plainly.

"Okay," he replied, his voice flat.

"Is there anything I can do to make you feel better?" I asked.

"No, but if you want to go drive my car and total it, that would seal the deal on my life."

I was done with him. I was not going to kiss his tail to make him feel better.

"Would you like to get something to eat?" I asked. "I will treat you."

"Actually, that would be nice," he said, and I couldn't find a bit of sarcasm in his response.

"Cool. Order what you like," I said.

Is dignity on the menu?" he asked.

"No, but I will check with the waiter," I said with my own sarcasm.

We ordered food, but there was no talking involved as we ate. I figured that we had exhausted all our talking points. And they only led back to the victim. I had had enough of that for the day.

When we had finished, I paid the tab, stood up from the table, and then exited the building. I didn't even say goodbye to Allen.

I was pretty sure that he didn't care.

He was a good example of why I was changing my business policy. In the future, I would take only women as clients. I didn't mind getting hit on by women, because I knew that it wasn't going anywhere.

Chapter 57

Keith's Epilogue

"Hey, Jennifer," I greeted as I walked to the front door of the bank branch.

"Hey, boss," she greeted back, and then she followed me down the hall and into my office.

I went behind my desk and sat down. I was in a somber mood. My life had gotten better, despite my awful choices. I was ever more grateful that I hadn't lost any of my friends. But something was still bothering me.

"Why do you look so sad?" Jennifer asked as she sat down in the chair in front of the desk. It was like it was her spot. She should have put a plaque with her name on it on that chair.

"I'm not sad. I'm happy. Just got a lot on my mind," I admitted.

"Well, you look like you need to get you some or just knock yourself off."

"Why is sex always on your mind?" I asked her point-blank.

"Because I love it." She grinned from ear to ear.

"There is a study that say that males think about sex more than women. I think you may be the wrong gender," I said and then chuckled.

"No, sir. I am all woman." She smoothed her hand all over her body in a seductive way.

"I have noticed that," I said and then laughed. "There is no doubt about it."

"I got a question for you." She sat up straight in the chair and looked me in the eyes.

"Oh, God," I uttered and then blew out my breath.

She wagged a finger at me. "Don't do that to me. I'm serious."

"Okay. What is it?" I asked.

"Do you miss Kingston?" she asked.

I looked at her without answering for a few seconds. "I miss parts of him," I confessed.

"What does that mean? *Parts* of him. You act like he has detachable parts or something."

"When I say, 'Parts of him,' I mean some of his personality," I explained.

"Like?" she asked.

"He was very charming, and he was handsome. He knew how to have adult conversations."

"If he had not tried to take you to the king, would you have tried to sleep with him?"

I laughed at her reference, but I had been truly scared he was going to kill me while I was lying on the floor that day, his big hands around my neck.

"He was married," was all I said. I purposely avoided answering the question.

But she didn't let me off the hook. "You didn't answer the question. Be honest."

"Yes, I would have," I said.

"It's hard to think that all the times you were in the office, he didn't try to get you on your knees." She laughed.

"I never said he didn't try. I said that he didn't succeed," I replied and then chuckled.

"Here you go with that wordplay," she said, and then she waved her hand at me like she was dismissing me.

"You need to ask better questions," I advised.

"Do you feel guilty about him losing his job?"

"Absolutely not. I didn't put my hands around my own neck in front of another employee. He put his hands around my neck and squeezed hard. I'm just glad that I wasn't alone at the time."

"Yes, honey, because he was not letting up. And you nearly passed out."

I instinctively put my hands on my neck. I hadn't slept well for weeks. I still woke up at night in a sweat and rubbing my neck.

"Yes, I can still feel his grip on my neck at times," I admitted out loud.

"But you got that promotion because of it."

"You know, I still feel guilty about that. That is not how I wanted to get promoted," I admitted.

"I wouldn't feel anything but my hands checking my bank account with a fresh raise." She guffawed.

"The money is nice, though. I'm not going to lie."

"I know yours is nice. The raise that they gave me will keep me here for at least another year or two." She laughed again. "But I will still complain, just to keep them on their toes."

The truth was, I still felt guilty about getting a promotion based on the fact that someone I had aligned myself with had tried to kill me because Jennifer had said something crazy to him to provoke him.

That was not the story we had told our superiors, but it came down to his story versus our story, and I had the marks on my neck to prove my story. Furthermore, other people in the office had said that he was on edge the whole time he was here that day. I didn't know what he'd been mad about, but I didn't care. They ended up letting Kingston go after a full investigation.

This wasn't a storybook ending, but I would take it.

Chapter 58

Justin's Epilogue

I was on the other side of the therapy table now. I was a patient now.

The fact that I had almost lost my life and was nonetheless on the road to recovery was a total miracle. I had spent two months in the hospital, fighting for my life. I had had multiple surgeries and procedures to correct my walking, talking, and breathing. I was glad to be out of the hospital, but I still had a long rehab road ahead of me.

When I saw that car coming full speed ahead as I sat on the restaurant patio, I thought that it was over for me and Marlon. I also thought that it was Angela behind the wheel. She had plenty of reasons to be. But the truth is, it was a true accident that the police investigated. They came to the resolution that the driver lost control of the car after a medical emergency.

Compared to me, Marlon was much further along in his healing process. He had to go through rehab too. He now used a cane to help him get around while recovering from his surgeries. He had suffered a broken leg and arm in the attack. I had broken both of my legs and two ribs and had had a punctured lung.

Marlon and I were still together.

When I'd woken from the coma that I was in, Marlon had been sitting right next to me, along with my close friends. He'd been in a wheelchair, though, so he'd needed help getting around. I was so glad that my friends liked him. They weren't too sure about the ex-wife and kid thing, but they had talked about that to me when we were alone. I was shocked when they hadn't harassed me about providing more details.

When I'd gone home from the hospital, Marlon had agreed to stay with me in my home and in the same bed. We hadn't worried about sex and all of that, because we were both not in any shape for that type of activity. Holding hands was more than enough.

My friends had been a big help. They'd taken turns getting me to therapy and sitting in the hospital room with me.

The biggest shock to me of all was Angela coming by the hospital to see Marlon and stopping by to see me too.

I felt guilty for misleading her, for convincing her that I cared about her well-being. I felt like such a jerk. I had intentionally misled her. Sometimes that was more painful than the accident.

Angela brought me to therapy sometimes too.

She was here with me now, as was Marlon.

She was a very loving person. I didn't know if I could be as strong as she was.

What kind of woman helped the boyfriend of her future ex-husband with his therapy sessions?

I knew that it couldn't be me. There was no way that I would help my ex-husband's boyfriend do anything. That would be too much of a stretch for me.

"Angela, thank you for helping me out today. It really means a lot. You are too good to me," I told her in a heartfelt manner.

"Justin, it is no problem. I love helping," she replied.

"You sure you are not trying to butter me up so that you can hurt me?" I said and then laughed.

"I'll let Marlon be the one to hurt you with his snoring," she said and then smiled.

"You know that you are right. He can suck up some sheets from the foot of the bed with his nose."

We both looked at him and then laughed.

"I almost put a pillow over his head the other night. I couldn't take it no more," I added.

"I'm not going to let you insult me right in front of me." Marlon got up out of the chair he was in and walked out of the room.

Angela and I shared another laugh.

We were the beginnings of a blended family, and I loved it.

I wasn't sure whether it was going to last or whether it would go left, but I was loving the time I was having with all the love and care that was in my corner.

Chapter 59

Marcus's Epilogue

I was so glad that my life had been spared in that motel room, all because the shooter didn't know how to put bullets in a gun. Melissa had had an illegal gun, and she was a novice with firearms.

I knew that Ronald was glad she didn't know how to shoot, because the gun had been aimed at his head instead of my own. I didn't know what her logic was when it came to making a decision about who would die and who would live.

"Doc, why would you do this to me?" she'd asked me as she stood there looking at Ronald and me, her hand with the gun in it now at her side.

"Melissa, it is hard to explain," I confessed. "I guess I like bad boys like you." I confessed, trying to lighten up the moment.

"I don't think that is a nice thing to say." She looked at me with indignation.

"I'm sorry, Melissa. That was not a good thing to say. I was trying to lighten the mood. I failed at it."

Her indignation melted. "You were right to say that. I just didn't want to hear it in this arena and right now. I am familiar with my life. I don't need it rehashed repeatedly. I made bad choices and lived with them." She walked over to one of the beds and sat down.

She threw the gun down beside her. Ronald and I both looked at it on the bed as it lay there. That gun was a game changer.

I was hoping that Ronald didn't try anything stupid, like going after that gun. I didn't trust him, and I knew that she didn't at all now.

She must have sensed us both eyeing the gun. She moved it closer to her. "You guys are lucky that I didn't know what I was doing, because one of you would have died and I would be on my way to jail right about now. All because you couldn't keep your hands to yourself."

"I'm sorry, baby. I made a mistake," Ronald responded.

"That's your problem. You make *tons* of mistakes. And you thought that your manhood was going to continue to blind me," she snapped. She glared at him. "How long was I supposed to be blind?"

She had made a valid point, and I was glad that she was having a breakthrough when it came to their relationship. I just didn't want it to be on my watch.

"I'm sorry, baby. It won't happen again. I need you." He almost sounded sincere. You just couldn't tell with his kind of guy, but I had my doubts.

"Tell me why I should trust you again?" she asked.

"You shouldn't," I chimed in.

Ronald looked at me like he wanted to murder me.

"Doc, are you saying that because you want him for yourself?" she asked, her gaze traveling over to me.

"Melissa, I wanted him for only one reason and one reason alone. Sex," I admitted.

"I think that I was doing the same thing. I wanted to build a relationship around his manhood, and that was not doable. It only keeps you for so long," she admitted.

"I know you two are not going to talk bad about me to my face." He looked like his feelings were hurt. But I didn't want to trust his feelings.

"Why not? You treated us badly to our faces. It is fitting that we are treating you now like you treated us. Game recognizes game," she replied coldly.

"I wasn't that bad. I know I had some moments. But y'all enjoyed yourselves. I didn't get any complaints." He gave a smile of satisfaction.

While he was right, I didn't want him to think he had one-upped us with his sexual prowess argument.

"Doc, are you trying to turn Melissa against me?" he asked, turning the spotlight on me.

"I could never do something that you do better than me," I answered. "I can't compete with you. You are a pro at taking advantage of people."

"I have to be good at something. God gave me these good looks, and you want me to just be a good guy. I tried that, and it didn't work out fast enough for me. I like results. Fast results," he replied. His words actually rang honest.

"Ronald, I think that it is best that you find yourself another victim to take advantage of," I responded. "Melissa is not going to fall for it anymore. Can't you tell? She was willing to take your life *and* go to jail for it. Why would you want to risk her trying that again? It would be insanity to put yourself through that. You would have to sleep with one eye open and be monitoring her to no end."

I shifted my gaze from Ronald to Melissa. "Melissa, why would you want to run a police station outside your home? There would be no moments of peace, just more manipulation and him treating you like a theme park. Do you want to be a roller coaster that goes every way but straight?"

They looked at each other in silence. I was hoping that these two people would come to their senses and walk away from each other.

It was the only way that I would be free. These two kind of deserved each other, but I wasn't going to unleash that kind of misery on the world or encourage it.

"Doc, you are right," Ronald said. "I don't want that kind of crazy going on. I will dip and let her be her. I won't be out here long before someone scoops me up." He was something else. He sure did need some therapy, because he was delusional.

"I am out of here," she said as she got up off the bed and placed the gun underneath her jacket. She exited the room as fast as she had entered it.

"So, it's just you and me now. You want to finish what we started?" He looked at me like I was actually going to entertain any chance of that.

"Roland, I am about to Zelle you some money, and then I want you to move on from me and Melissa. Why don't you try to be an adult and start living on your own?"

He looked at me and then laughed loudly. "That's a good one, Doc. But I'm a user, and I will always be one." He walked past me, and I watched him go out of the room without turning back.

Minutes later, I exited the motel room, walked outside and got in my car.

"Please God let me be free from them forever," I prayed aloud as I turned the key in the ignition.

As I drove home from that life-changing experience, I decided I wanted to do something entirely
new with my life. I didn't know exactly what yet,
but I knew that I would sooner or later discover a
different career path.

While I hadn't liked going through any of this, it
had brought me a change of heart.

I was going to jump out there and enjoy this
world.

Me and my boys. Us against the world.

The End